Bejesus

Lukas Allen

Lukas Allen

Contents

1

"As such a… new… practitioner, you get a princess wand." a girl called Abbot said.

The other girls smirked at me, as I begrudgingly took my new wand.

What fucking bullshit!! I could light them all on fire with one hand and roast sausages on them for days!!

The Madame, a middle aged woman, saw that look in my eyes, and said, "Now, Mary… You need a talisman if you want to channel your-"

"It's Jane. Mary Jane." I said.

And I saw that look in *her* eyes, and she snapped at me, saying, *"You are what I call you. No matter* what *your lineage… We will not bow down to* you."

I stared into her eyes, as the sparks seemed to fly off of us.

Shit, a spark actually did fly off of me, and set fire to the curtains.

The Madame sighed, and said, "Someone please douse that, and then you can all go to bed."

"I can use her blood, if you like." the girl who gave me the wand, Abbot, said.

"No, no… just find *something,* because I really can't stand another fire… The smoke upsets my lungs…" the Madame said, walking away.

The other girls put out the flame, and I went to bed.

Why did I ever take upon this... *slavery*. School is supposed to be drinkin' and partying! And what the fuck am I going to do with a degree in *magic??*

I sighed, snuggled in my bed in our shared room, and looked at the drawing my boyfriend, my artist, gave me before I left.

It was a picture of him smiling and winking, with one thumb up, with the words "Good luck!" above it. I sneakily kissed the drawing, hoping no one would notice-

Abbot appeared before me, decloaking from invisibility, snatching my drawing.

"Who's this?? Your boytoy??" she said.

"Give it back." I said, trying to snatch the drawing from her.

"Oops." she said, and burned the picture in her hand.

I was pale in fury, and was about to beat the shit out of her-

But she cackled, and said, "For the *Devil's Daughter* you sure have no class... Oh wait. That's to be expected, isn't it? What are you going to do if you kill *me??* There's nothing you can do. You'll be expelled, killed yourself... and then everything you've ever loved will be gone. Just like this pic."

I put down my fists, and sat back down on the bed.

She walked away, muttering to herself, calling me a stupid bitch.

I thought this might be a good place for me to hone my skills... I was practically a pyromancer, in some degree... I could roast things alive, just because of my "lineage."

I was Mary Jane, and I was the Devil's Daughter.

And now I was just some idiot abroad, in a strange school in a strange place... filled with stupid wiccan bitches.

God, I was too old for this shit. And too young to worry about this shit, too. I was in that cusp of hellish adulthood where I was either stuck fulfilling my calling, or stuck always dreaming about it.

I *wanted* to just be stronger, I wanted to take the world by storm. I felt special, and my boyfriend made me feel special, as he drew me naturally in my glorious nudity.

I know what you're thinking, that sounds weird, but it's fun having someone appreciate your natural form, if you know what I mean.

I sighed, and wished I could tell him that... We'd get our phones back for an hour at the end of the week.

I just put my stupid princess wand by my bedside, and went to sleep.

We'd have to work early in the morning... God, I wish there was somewhere better to learn magic than an actual brothel in Holland...

I woke up in the morning, took a communal shower and brushed my teeth, and then went to work.

I didn't work "hands on." It was each girl's choice what job we did in the house...

Abbot was a filthy slut. And now she was a professional whore.

Some of the more educated girls worked promotions, the books, and all sorts of other side businesses, the Madame was the head, and taught us what she knew about the darker forces when she could. A few of the very street educated girls were drug dealers and hook up specialists.

And I was the maid.

I picked up Abbot's disgusting stained clothes as she smoked a cigarette, as she was nude after fulfilling another "job."

"Spritz down the chair, too. He sat on it for a bit." Abbot said.

I sighed, and spritzed down the chair.

"Y'know... You could really do well, on your back... Want me to teach you?" Abbot said, smirking.

"No, I think I'm fine, thanks. Oh God- What is that?" I said, looking at something disgusting in the sheets.

Abbot laughed, and said, "Beats me. Dude was practically a leper, with things falling off him left and right. C'mon... Don't you want to please your mistress in between her break?" and she spread her thighs for me.

I looked at her, disgusted.

"You *never* thought about being with a woman? Even just as a sub?" Abbot said, closing her legs.

I silently cleaned up the rest of the room, and Abbot was about to touch me.

I snatched her wrist before she could feel a tit.

Abbot shrugged, and opened the door, where someone absolutely... disgusting, walked in.

I guess they all looked disgusting, to me.

"Two for one. Nice." he said.

I quickly left the room out the back.

2

I felt sick. Abbot was making love to a dog in front of an audience. And I had to clean it up.

We were the back alley hookers, the prostitutes, the end of all dreams.

And I was the maid, the Devil's Daughter.

But there was something so tantalizing about the other half... Real magic. Spectacular, unadulterated dreams, that you could wave your hand and make whatever you want appear.

There wasn't even a dog out there, just some sort of illusion.

But the thing about illusions... and I don't think I'll ever understand this, but they make just as much of a mess as real life.

The people applauded. The curtain closed. The illusion disappeared. And I set to work.

I thought I'd throw up, but Abbot just smoked a cigarette as the next girl came out.

Abbot passed me by, and said, "Ol' Rover really got 'em goin', eh? Makes me wonder about the real thing... What do you know about dog fucking, degenerate Devil's Daughter? Maybe you can give me some tips."

I ignored her, as she laughed.

There was all sorts of scuzz that you could find, most of it was even conveniently legal in some "special" places. You'd think the legality of it would make it less of a taboo, less practiced... but there will always be "special" places populated with "special" people.

There was a real actor and an actress next up, for that is what they were, acting out the scenes of love on stage. He looked frankly very into it. Poor guy... he seemed new.

I tried to warn him to back out of here after, but all I got out of him was drug filled metaphors. He was stoned.

Stupid idiot. He took the bait, fell for the trap, and they used him up like a condom then thrown in the trash.

You'd think it's only the women, the whores, who are the victims of this sort of business... but really, the victim was the consumer.

And they fell for it with a smile, most of the time knowing the illusion and eating the fruit of desire anyway.

It was a big market, in Holland. Commercial lovemaking. Tourists would spend thousands of dollars on one night with a professional lovemaker, and had been looking forward to it all their lives.

What? Do you think that's expensive? Love is priceless.

And these were professionals at it.

I cleaned up room after room, princess wand at my side. I barged into one that was being used, by accident, and the other girl told me to leave, but the guy said, "No. Let her stay. I want her to see this."

The prostitute looked back at me, and nodded.

The man called me his wife, as he ejaculated on the prostitute.

I left quickly.

The next room I had to clean up BDSM... leftovers. Gosh, that was a lot of blood...

But I found a neat little whip... and I was going to pocket it, maybe as a souvenir. I actually kinda liked this stuff.

I looked at the cruel, snake's head... and it kind of reminded me of my home.

I ditched it as soon as I could. *That was not my home.*

My home was back, well, home. With my artist.

It took me a while to find this place… but Luke, the silly goof, had actually stumbled upon here by accident before he met me. He spent fifty euros on a handjob. Said it wasn't worth it, and also, well, couldn't finish like that with some stranger.

They *were* all just strangers, the lovemakers, but they harp on making you think they're that special kind of stranger that you always wanted to meet. The ones who liked you, anyway.

They could pick and choose. If you weren't her type, she'd slam the door in your face. Usually their types were the big spenders, and not bums, like Luke was.

Fifty euros on a handjob… heh. His last fifty, as well. Then he spent his last five euros in coins on a train ticket to the airport, completely broke, in shame for failing at his dream of living abroad.

I thought it was a pretty cool story, when he told me, the whole ups and downs of travelling, living like a carefree traveller, going most of the places you could on your own two feet.

I was a different kind of traveller. My journey was through the very ether of reality.

By the end of the week I saw most of the idiots on their flight back home, smiling in happiness with full bellies, sated desires, and empty pockets.

The one idiot who really got reeled into the business already had the cold look in his eye, as he did the same act over and over on stage, although he'd soon learn to hide that… or else he'd have even less.

The Madame caught me before I had finished everything up.

"You will *straighten* as you clean. If I catch you hunched over and falling down, I will use that whip you misplaced on you instead." the Madame said.

"I don't know where it went. I put it… somewhere." I said.

She did not slap me. She was much too composed, even to take my cheek.

She said, "Then I will show you something else, than cheek."

I looked at her. I blinked. She had read my mind.

And as she looked into my eyes, her eyes turned black… and she showed me what was in her mind.

I started screaming, in a second.

She wasn't hurting me.

She was scaring me.

Th-The tentacles. Th-The teeth…

And the cold look.

This was not a human being, this person.

This was not even a demon.

It was worse… It was the horrible transition between the two.

"I am the Madame, to you, and you will remember that before you call me some horrible pronoun like 'it.'" the Madame said, and walked away.

3

I called Luke at the end of the week.

"Jane! How are you? Everything going well?" he said.

"Yeah, I think I can learn a lot here... how to clean up ejaculation..." I said, and sighed.

"...You know you can come back. I know you took this journey to find out more about yourself, but you can always come home whenever you like. I wish I was there." he said.

"Nah, you don't. You wouldn't, anyway. This stuff... it seems kind of neat on the surface, but underneath it's just... egh, you get sick of it." I said.

"Yeah, I can understand that... That's why I always tried to keep my art on the classy side-" he said.

"With naked butts and boobs! But my butt and boobs. Man... I wish you could see what I'm doing right now..." I said, grinning.

He said, "Oohlala. I wish I could... I'll get the pens and pencils, and stroke down a line or two what I envision you doing..."

I giggled. We had blatant phone sex pretty soon, but only words. We both just enjoyed the talk even over stimulation. It's the memory of it which gets you later, anyway.

"Whooph! Gosh, but all that aside, have they even taught you *any-thing* yet??" Luke said, when he hit a nice stopping point.

"I learned I need a talisman. It's a pink, plastic wand with a sparkly star on the top." I said.

"...Is that a joke? Shouldn't it be Rasputin's tailbone, or something?" he said.

I sighed, and said, "No... I guess not. I think it was just a prank, honestly. If nothing changes I'll ditch this dump... but I did meet my worst nightmare. She's my teacher and my boss."

"...Yikes. Well, don't take her cheek, if you don't have to. We've seen what's worse than anything, before." he said.

"Yeah, my dad gets a bad rap, but really... There is so much worse than the fallen angel of Hell. We demonize people who are, well, like the Devil... but I believe there is always new evil, in every dark, horrible cranny of the world, and even things beyond." I said.

"That's a good point. I believe some of it is even in ourselves. Like my voices... they're-" he said.

"Are they starting up again?" I asked.

"I just get stressed with some things, and they tend to pop up when things aren't perfect." he said, "Like you being gone."

"Aww, shucks. Quit being so dreamy, and I'll see you in your dreams again sometime." I said.

"...You can still do that?" he asked.

"Well, it's difficult now... I frankly feel very strange in my head, like it's a giant labyrinth, especially in my dreams. Old monsters that take on new personas pop out, and sometimes little fears turn into giant nightmares. Have any good dreams, lately?" I asked.

"No... I had a dream of my old middle school teacher, smiling like a madwoman..." he said.

"Doesn't sound so bad." I said, "Was it a wet dream, or somethin'?"

"...No. It was terrifying." he said.

I laughed, and said, "What did you do to get out of it? I didn't know middle school teachers were a fear for you."

He laughed, and said, "They are when they're chasing me with a demented smile on their face. I woke myself up."

"...How?" I asked.

"Beats me. Open your eyes? Hmm... I guess I just looked the monster in the eyes, felt that tremoring fear, and reset the dream by opening my eyes in the dark." he said.

"...Cool. I'll try that next time." I said.

We talked a little more, just about big things or little things, but eventually I said, "I love you, Luke. I'll see you soon when this is over."

"I love you too, Mary Jane." he said.

I slowly hung up, and then gave my phone back to the Madame, as I was already broaching upon the end of our phone time.

I went to bed.

I had a dream of endless locked doors, keys, heart shaped locks...

None of the keys I had were the right one. I knew Luke was behind one of these... but which?

I tried listening to his voice, but it was only silence.

And the monster was chasing me. I could feel it, but I couldn't see it, and I knew in a dream once you get paranoid it'll show up.

I walked down the hall, past the endlessly locked doors...

I opened a door that wasn't locked.

I walked into Abbot's mind.

"I was waiting for you." Abbot said, snapping the snake whip.

I stepped back aways, but there was no door behind me to walk out of.

"You're filthy. A filthy Devil's Daughter... and it's time you learned your lesson.

"Do you think I *like* doing what I do?? Catering to the filth?? There's so much more I could be doing with my time...

"And now we have *you* here... The archnemesis of creation's daughter.

"I'm going to hurt you now." Abbot said.

She snapped the whip at me, I looked her in the eyes…

But she snickered, and said, "This dream is what I always wanted to do to your master… Now I'm going to do it to you."

She snapped me with the whip, and it hurt.

Pain! I needed to-

Pinch myself? She was already snapping me over and over with the whip, my bare skin bleeding…

So I used fire.

I lit everything *everywhere* on fire.

I woke up in my bed to the smoke, and another girl putting me out with a fire extinguisher.

"Fucking hell. You need to learn control." the girl said.

"Thank you." I said.

"…Don't mention it. We're all in this together." she said, and everyone went back to bed, as I went to get new sheets that weren't almost all ashes and covered in foam.

I bumped into Abbot, who was also getting bedsheets for her bed.

"Don't you *dare* trigger me, Devil's Daughter." Abbot said. She smelled like smoke.

I smirked. I knew how to inject a good idea in someone's head with a dream… and I knew how to set things on fire… So Abbot set herself on fire, at my behest.

4

In the morning I cleaned up the one girl who put me out with the fire extinguisher's office, even though it was pretty spotless.

She worked the books, and frankly got us working with no hassle from the government, not even taxes.

She was sharpening pencils with a knife, and said, "You know, burning your bed is the equivalent of wetting it for one of us."

I sighed, bagged up the trash, and said, "Yeah, I figured... It's just-"

"It's a good escape route, though. Abbot can really be a snarky one, when she doesn't like you." she said, continuing to sharpen pencils.

"...So what do I do?" I asked.

"Like any bully, you show them their place. I don't know how you're going to do that with that wand at your waist... Seems like a joke, but it'll make you, and us, stronger with your pain.

"I want you to choose the object on my desk which is the strongest talisman for me. Choose correctly, and I'll let you keep it." she said, putting down the knife on the desk.

The... knife? That was physically the strongest object... It looked sharp, in great condition, and if it was the talisman, then I could keep it, to protect myself...

I sighed, and pointed at a pencil.

"Bravo!" the woman said, "A strong magical object isn't always the one that can hurt the most. And frankly... my pencils do more than any stupid knife. Take one, and work on your power."

I took a pencil, and said, "Thanks. I'm-"

"Yeah, yeah, Mary. I'm Francesca. Pleasure to meet you, Maid Marian." she said, smirking and shaking my hand.

In my smoke break, I waved the pencil in the air, hoping it would do something... magical.

It was just a pencil.

I shrugged. My artist always found pencils handy, although preferred to draw and write in black pen.

I drew something down for him, when the day was up.

I put all my passion, my longing, my sadness, anger, and then the happiness of seeing his face down as it came out of the pencil, and then...

The picture moved. I was watching him eating pancakes. He looked kind of sad.

"Luke! Can you hear me?? How are you?" I said.

He frankly started to look very paranoid, and finished his pancakes, and left the picture.

I sighed, as I had drawn a picture of an empty table in a diner.

I drew him walking down the street, passing the intersection, going down the road... and the pictures all moved.

And I drew him meeting a woman.

I stopped drawing, and the pictures stopped as he hugged her.

I couldn't see the woman's face, but I scratched up her entire body.

So. That was the way of it.

Leave home, and home leaves me.

I screamed in anger and... sadness.

I continued to draw, trying to figure out who this woman was. There was always a strand of hair over her face, as she wore a hood. Who *was* she??

Was it Lily? Kayla? Jill? All those old bitch friends of mine... I knew he must be seeing one of them!!

He- He brought her home. To *our* home.

I didn't have the heart to draw anymore.

Huh. And he said all those nice things over the phone. Was this his plan??

Just because I'm the *Devil's Daughter* doesn't mean I deserved this!! Could he really not wait just a few months??

Fucking slut. The both of them. When this is over, I'll come back with my full power and *burn them to smithereens...*

I heard him saying all those loving things, in my mind. I practically could hear them right by my ear... Him saying...

"You're my heart, and I am yours, beating just for you..."

It's the memory that really gets you, anyway.

5

I felt powerless. I could do nothing, not even bitch at him over the phone.

I set back to work the next day. I made mistakes, and was hounded relentlessly by the Madame.

I didn't really care, all that I really cared about was this horrid feeling in my stomach.

I ate our food, which was actually quite good since we had our own chef, and it was tasteless to me.

I had one person who was really sorta my friend. We just ate together. She was one of the drug dealers, and could easily be mistaken for a man if you looked at her wrong.

"You want them pancakes? I like a good pancake." she said.

I gave her the pancakes.

She, Tas, said, "You really gotta learn Dutch, man, because then the country will open up to you, like, really. We have the best pannenkoeken huizen in the world."

"You're one of the few of us who is actually from here. What's the point of learning Dutch if I'm never going to get out of this house?" I said.

"You'll feel less trapped? Fuck if I know, but it's a great way to open up your mind. Once you get into the whole language of the world, then you can really see colors, describe them in different ways, quite differently, just with the many words you know for the color blue. Blauw, like you look." she said, and smiled gently to me.

"Is magic always correct? Does it make mistakes?" I asked.

"It is always correct, for the appropriate occasion. That may not be correct for someone else. If you're asking if it will always aid you... it may, if that is what you want of it." she said.

"But I saw my boyfriend cheat on me, in a magic picture." I said.

She shrugged, "Some States guy? Probably would, right? Maybe that's what you needed to know."

I looked down at my food, and picked at a strawberry with my fork.

I then ditched work, on a really stupid reason.

I claimed I was going to mass.

The Madame heartily allowed me to, saying that religion has some of the most magical power of all, and if I could I should learn from it as well and seduce it to my will to harness it.

I was going to just bum around and drink, and that's what I did. I was super drunk, with a couple cool Italians flirting with me, when I decided I might as well go to mass.

Fuck if I gave a shit about religion. I wasn't Christian, and proud of it, unlike Luke.

Stupid Christians. Maybe I'll just burn the church down.

I kissed the Italians on the cheek, exchanged numbers even though I couldn't use my phone, and went to mass alone.

I sat in the back row, as the priest droned on and on in a sermon, drowning me in some Dutch I couldn't even understand.

I went to communion, why not, and ate the stupid bread that was so unfulfilling.

I drank a lot of the wine.

And then... I thought I'd bitch at the priest, because he didn't do one cool thing in the entire mass. When Luke brought me to a mass before, the priest actually had props, little rubber ducks, and made jokes. This guy was booooring.

I sat in the confession box, and said, "Iiii want to confesssss... that you're stupid."

"...Are you an American?" he asked.

"Duhhhh. Stupid... Soooo stupid..." I said.

"...Do you have anything else to confess?" he said.

"Yeahh. My boyfriend is stupidddd, too. He probably won't be my boyfriend much longeeeer, when I do what he did to meeee... but with *two* lovers. Hahaha... Take that." I said.

"...I see. And you feel bad for this?" he said.

"...Fuck, I don't know. But shouldn't it be like a dick for a dick, or sommme bullshit? Take two for him fucking some slut?" I said.

"I think revenge never solves anything really. I believe that forgiveness is the goal we should strive for." he said.

"Whaaat... God tell you that, or something?" I said.

"In a way of speaking. In that feeling of goodness I get, when I absolve sins, even just sins against me." he said.

"Fuckin'... fine. Absolve me. Do your stupid duty, stupid." I said.

"In the name of the Father, Son, and Holy Spirit, I absolve your sins. Say ten Hail Marys in penance." he said.

"Fuck... I'll say one. Ok? Then I'm gonna sin some more." I said.

"...Do you know the words?" he said.

"Haily Mary, slut amongst us, you're a cunt and you look like a duck, go out amongst us, and go fuck. That right?" I said.

He sighed, and said, "Just follow along with me."

I sighed, and we said the Hail Mary. Stupid Mary... probably just like my dead mother named Mary, too.

I was going to leave after using the bathroom of the church, throwing up quite a bit actually, and washed the puke bits I accidentally got on my hands in the sink, and I saw her in the mirror.

I saw the bitch that Luke was seeing.

I only saw me, but I knew somehow that he wouldn't cheat on a fancy. I couldn't really explain it, but that's what I felt.

I went back home, not going to the Italians' place, and drew again with my magic pencil.

I drew the woman under the hood.

She was a nun, a friend of mine actually.

She was laughing in the picture, looking happy.

Luke hugged her goodbye, and she waved back at him. They both had rosaries in their hands.

Luke placed the rosary back on the mantle.

And looked into my eyes in the picture, and winked.

Fucking asshole!! He was just praying a stupid rosary with my nun??

I laughed, looking at his silly still picture of him winking eternally.

6

He did say he always hated praying the rosary, but maybe it was helpful for him.

I didn't care why he prayed those stupid beads, I felt so relieved.

I saw Abbot's rosary on her bunk.

What a bitch. Christians think they're all nice and kind and loving, but they can have just as much hate as anyone. Abbot was just prejudiced against the Devil. Fucking asshole.

I heard her talking to Francesca as they were smoking a bit aways outside and I had come out for a cig.

"...so that's that. He's finally leaving the order and marrying my mother- Oh. The Devil bitch is here." Abbot said.

I walked up to them, lighting my cigarette, and said, "I want to settle this, Abbot. You're not going to push me around anymore."

Abbot laughed harshly, and Francesca said, "I think you should-"

Abbot said, "Quiet, bookworm. Devil bitch wants to learn, so I'm going to teach her."

Abbot then flicked a finger, and I fell to the ground.

It took all I had to get back up. Even just my hair was extremely heavy.

I wielded my princess wand, and shot sparks at her. It smelled like burning plastic, but the princess wand held.

She blew it back at me with a puff of air, and sparks flew in my eyes.

She tackled me to the ground, and began punching me in the face.

"This. Is. How. You. Fight!! You don't throw your idiotic powers in my face, thinking you can take me!! I don't even need magic!! And you're gonna bleed." she said, thumping me over and over on the nose, making me bleed.

I felt so angry, as I was bleeding and hurting.

I stared into her eyes.

And I realized I should never take this. I was who I was, and not a punching bag.

I felt like my old self, who burned people's homes down because I thought it was funny.

The horns ruptured from my head, and I jammed them into Abbot's chest.

Francesca bound me with a swish of her pencil, invisible chains that held me down as Abbot was gasping on my side and bleeding from her chest.

Francesca said, "You've done enough, Mary. I think you should learn composure, as well as strength. You do not blatantly kill your foe. You let them suffer.

"And Abbot… Would your father really like to finally have that family he's dreamed of with you dying? Take heedence to your own mortality, and realize the more you push, the more others will push back.

"I have just alerted the Madame, and you will both be lucky to stay. With increased responsibilities.

"She just told me herself."

We were taken to our beds, and Abbot was treated as she moaned from being impaled on my horns, and my nose was treated.

Our nurse was actually the most experienced doctor in the world, purely because she had an edge on all mundane society. She used magic.

"Don't know what I can do about the horns… but your nose is fine. And quit whining, Abbot, you're not getting my pain pills since you're completely fine too now." the nurse said, and walked away.

Abbot grumbled, and clutched her rosary.

I said, even though I didn't *want* to, but I thought it might avoid an encounter like this again, "Sorry, Abbot. I was really going to try to kill you if you didn't back off. I don't care what would've happened to me."

She snarled at me, and began praying.

I stared at her praying the rosary, and hazarded to ask, "…So you go to church? I talked to a real stupid priest while I was there. It felt dumb, but I guess it helped."

She stopped praying for a second, looked into my eyes, and said, "That priest *is* dumb. Flunked out of college, and joined the ministry. He's my father's replacement, and I wish they picked someone who is at least easier on the eyes…"

"Your father?" I asked.

"He's a priest. That's right. I'm a minister's daughter. And I'm proud of it." she said.

"…Is that what you were talking about to Francesca earlier?" I said.

"Yeah. So? He's finally going to be my real dad and marry my mother. That's all I ever wanted of him. Stupid Catholics take a vow, break the vow, and then give up on a real committment, to be a father. He kept me secret for so long, as my mother did, but… he said it was the biggest regret of his life. I actually threatened to expose him for it… and he thanked me.

"Said he finally heard the Lord's will, and that it came out of my mouth." she said.

"…So why are you here? We're like witches, or something, right?" I said.

"That's *such* an out of date term. It's mostly synonymous with bitch, even rhymes with it. I prefer to think of us as practitioners. Some of you, like *you*, practice dark stuff. I practice the magic of God." she said.

"...But I saw you give head to a-" I said.

"And it was the Lord's will. Do not question my actions, unless you want me to question yours as well." Abbot said.

"...Point taken. You think we can make a truce? I mean, I get what you meant about not having a dad. My dad's the Devil. Now I don't want him to be my father, unlike you. I understand it is hard to find your family." I said.

She sighed, and said, "It is hard to trust you with horns growing out of your head. Feels evil. But ok, for now. Don't cross me again."

7

The Madame was teaching us a lesson, and she taught us newbies simple clarity.

The Madame said, "There is a simple way of clarity, when you look, you will see, when you seek, you shall find. This is for evil, good, or what's in between."

Abbot said, "Just like the Lord's will-"

"Quiet. Something else may seek you, as well, and they will find, unless you are clear of mind. You must always search yourself to find truth, because sometimes you do not want what you want, and should approach what you need, instead. Seek clarity of vision, with an open mind, soul, and body. I will now allow you to practice, please take a partner and search for their strength, and you shall find your own as well."

I paired up with- Shit. I guess Abbot was the only one available.

She sighed, as I sat across from her, and said, "I find sexual acts to find the most open parts of people. Would you like to try that? I hurl at the thought of kissing you, but if the Madame insists..."

"Er, no. I think we should... hold hands? Is that how we do this?" I said.

The Madame was staring me hard in the eyes as I looked back at her, watching, waiting.

I quickly held hands with Abbot, to get the Madame's gaze off of me.

We closed our eyes, and I tried to seek for Abbot's strength.

She *was* strong, that much was obvious. She was… good at her job, one of the most popular prostitutes here. She was-

But she was lost.

I saw her in my mind, looking for something, and like her father, like her God, she could not find it.

Although I saw her find something else I was seeking for.

She said in our minds, "This is the door you're seeking for. I don't know *how* it wasn't obvious. It screams out for you, unlike the rest."

I looked at the heart locked door.

"How do I open it?" I said.

"Help me first, and I'll-" she said.

"You don't even know how to open the door." I said.

"…Screw you! You just burn it, or something!" she said.

"…But it's made of metal." I said.

"I don't care! Help me find my puppy! He disappeared when I was young, and that's what I really want. My dad and my God can come at their own pace… Really I just care about what happened to my dog!! It's been driving me crazy most of my life!

"Do you think my neighbor stole it?? Was it hit by a car?? Did he just run off??" she said.

"I think you've been looking too long for a lost dog, and that it represents the other stuff you were looking for as well." I said.

"God, you're stupid. He was my best friend, and you don't leave a friend, even if they get killed or something. You avenge them." she said, crossing her arms.

I thought about what could've happened to Abbot's dog. It was driving me crazy eventually, too.

I sighed, and said, "Well, you know he's dead. You had him when, if I'm reading you correctly, when you were five?"

"…So?" she said.

"So I think it doesn't matter how hard you look, he's passed on. You won't have him how you remember him, and it would be wise to put him to rest." I said.

"...Ok. I guess... Doesn't mean he wasn't the best dog ever, still. I suppose I should let him go, up to the sky in Heaven, instead of keeping him locked in my heart..." she said.

Locked in my heart?

Was I the only one keeping this door locked?

I lit my hand in fire, and placed it in the keyhole.

It opened up, as I let go.

And Luke was there, smiling to me...

With so many other people shouting and screaming at him in his head.

I told them all to shush, and took him out of the room, with me.

We walked down the halls of locked doors, and went home.

I opened my eyes, and Abbot was crying.

"I... I'm so sorry, Maarty... I'm so sorry you're dead..." she said.

I squeezed her hands, looked back at the Madame, and she was smiling.

The Madame said, "True strength can be found if you stop looking, and accept the truth."

8

"Um. Tas... I- I didn't know. I'm sorry." I said to my drug dealer friend, you know, the one who could be mistaken for a man.

She sighed, and pulled back up her pants. "I'm sorry, Mary. I just thought- Thought that maybe-"

"It's ok. I think you're great, and you'll find someone soon, too." I said, stroking her cheek.

She touched my hand, and said, "I know. I was hoping it would be you."

I put my hand back to my side, and said, "Well. It sure is a good looker. Maybe- You know- That one guy-"

She sighed, and said, "No, I don't think so. He's a real prick when you get to know him. I don't know... I like some, I like others... but this one girl... hooboy. She just really gets me. She's from Belgium."

"I think you'll be able to work things out." I said.

I hugged Tas in the room we were in that I was cleaning.

She said, "Just because I have a penis, don't think differently of me, ok? I *like* being a woman. It's... magical. It's my one biggest regret, that I don't know how to transmute it right... besides going to some hack plastic surgeon."

"That's always an option, and who knows, maybe if you learn enough you'll be able to do so right." I said.

Tas smiled, and said, "Thanks. It's the hope of that which keeps me going. Well... I'll see you. Please don't tell anyone else."

I smiled gently, and said, "It's our secret. I always did wonder why you didn't live on our 'campus...'"

"Private parts, private bathroom. It keeps the girls thinking I'm one of them... It makes me sad, honestly, hiding myself. But I'll keep doing so, if I get the acceptance I have been getting." Tas said.

She left, and went out to score her next drug deal.

I smiled. Tas is gonna be so lucky, when she finds someone who likes her for who she is. It didn't matter what genitalia she had, she would find that someone eventually.

I decided to try to fix her dilemma.

I worked on a dead chicken, one from out back that died of some sickness.

I tried to change its genitalia, from male to female parts. Stupid rooster, why won't you be a female...

I tried to draw it down, with my pencil, as a female chicken, but it was still dead.

I tried to find what it was looking for, with clarity, but it was still dead.

I thought... hmm... Its problem was being dead. What if I simply found its soul? My dad stole souls, what if I just stole this rooster's soul back into its body?

I meditated, and I communed.

The spirits were silent, as they were ever since I came back to the living world, but I looked for this rooster, even cradling its corpse on my lap.

I found it, as I walked through millions of souls of other dead roosters.

I picked him up gently, and brought him back to his body.

Now all I had to do was somehow sculpt its genitals into female parts!

The rooster corpse moved.

I jumped back. Shit.

It cockadoodle dooed in a rather horrible manner.

It followed me back into the house, as I tried to lose it.

Another girl jumped back, and said, "Th-That's not right."

"It's ok, Malena. I don't really know how, but I-" I said.

"You're not supposed to *do* that!! That's like- advanced stuff! It's only for the Madame!!" Malena said.

I looked at her quizzically, and said, "Was pretty easy. Sorry for barging in, that one time."

"No w-worries. S-Some guys really get a k-kick out of cheating on th-their wives, and he t-tipped me well... We need to get rid of this." Malena said

"...Why?" I said, as the dead, rotting rooster picked itself for fleas.

"...I'm going to tell the Madame, and we'll-" she said.

"Please!! She's such a ballbreaker!! I'll do whatever you want, just don't get me in trouble again." I said.

"...We're going to let it out into the forest. To live life as a natural rooster. Yeah." Malena said.

I picked up the rotting rooster, and we got into Malena's car. She drove quickly, she drove carefully, but eventually we got to a natural park.

She said, "...Now kill it, or let it go, or whatever. I never want to even think of this again."

I shrugged, took out the rooster, and let it go.

It stood there, looking at me.

"...Go on. Go be a rooster." I said.

It cockadoodle dooed in that horrible manner, and walked off.

I waved my little Frankenstein goodbye, sad that I couldn't turn it into a female.

Later in the day, Malena was silently mouthing "sorry" to me as the Madame called me into her office.

"I understand you've been playing with life and death." the Madame said, as I sat down.

"...I was just trying to turn a cock into a pussy. Sorry." I said.

"...No one has the power over life, Mary. Only one man I knew had that strength... and he was Jesus Christ." the Madame said.

I blinked. The Madame knew Jesus?

"Of course I did. I've aged rather well... but he was a friend of mine... a long time ago..." the Madame said.

Who *was* this strange person??

"I am the Madame, to you. I honestly don't know what to do about this. I have tried, agelessly, to bring my friends, lovers, family, back to life, but all I get is their spirits screaming at me in their- my head. What is it you want to do about the life you've brought back to the world?" the Madame said.

"Beats me. Isn't it just a chicken? It'll be dead soon eventually, since we let it out in the forest..." I said.

She laughed.

"That is the way of life, is it not? Perhaps I am thinking too hard on this... We will hone this skill of yours, and learn what to do about it eventually. Perhaps we can start the apocalypse, eh? Claim you as Jesus come down as a woman? It would be nice to have an end to this world..." the Madame said.

I blinked. I said, "But I'm the Daughter of the Devil..."

"Exactly. I listen to the signs... and when you contacted me with that email, I knew I must respond to this harbinger, you, and treat her to true knowledge. I believed this would take longer, but the horns on your head already show a deeper plot than I could understand from the surface.

"So I ask you this. What is it you want to do? This facility's services are now completely open to you." the Madame said.

"...Um... Can you teach me how to- Maybe I can learn- I at least don't want to be a maid anymore. Can't I do *anything* else?" I said.

She smiled, and said, "The young are so disoriented... Very well. You seem to dislike our work, at best, but perhaps you can work at the bar I opened up across the street. Drunken spenders love a lay in the hay... and perhaps we can use your 'charm' and 'influence' to send them here."

I smiled, and said, "Thank you. Can I please ask you... what's your real name? I'm just curious, is all."

"Magdalene. I believe the name 'Mary' causes much too much confusion, sometimes. But to you, I am the Madame. Here are the keys to the bar... work well, and I'll show you how to transmute water to beer. Jesus taught me that trick himself." the Madame said, and handed me some keys.

I took them in happiness, awaiting a job I could finally be proud of.

I worked the bar, most of the time, and it was pretty fun-

This guy just felt my boobs.

He drunkenly grinned at me, with his tourist friends laughing and one saying, "Look! Joe got a demon girl girlfriend!!"

I lit them on fire.

Soon the bar was all ablaze, with me standing outside of the bar.

9

Luke and I made out in our conjoined dreams. I was going to do more with Luke, but I stopped him, as my breathing was so heavy, heaving up and down, and said, "No, wait. If we do more we'll wake up."

"Ok. It's too bad you're not really with me, but I like what you did with the scenery. You're an artist at heart." Luke said, admiring my dream canvas.

We were in the middle of a beautiful forest, beside a roaring river with rainbows draping the sky.

"I was actually worried it might be too sappy. You know I'm not really accustomed to this sort of setting." I said, as we sat back up on the picnic blanket.

He shrugged, and said, "You can always dream."

Then I heard giggling coming from behind us, and I yelled out, "Who's there? It better not be some sort of succubus."

Abbot walked out from the forest, and said, "Much worse. Pleased to meet you, Mary's boytoy! What a... quaint, spot for a picnic!" and she shook Luke's hand as we were seated.

I sighed, and said, "Don't you have dream dogs to fuck?"

Abbot shrugged, and said, "Nah. I was just wondering if you were going to burn your bed again, and I see you might, with this hottie... my, my, my..."

Luke blushed, and I said, "Oh, quit the act. Don't try to seduce every man you see, or you'll probably get seven years bad luck or something."

Abbot sat beside us, and said, "Not an act. I loooove the Americans. They're so- well, you're not as tall as us Nederlanders, Luke, but you've definitely got that American masculinity!"

"Yeah. You love them until you're just trying to serve them beer and then they grope you… Fucking asshole tourists. Can't they treat our home better?" I said.

"Your home?" Luke said.

"Well, if I'ma live here, I'ma make it a home. It'll save time for me. You know I miss our apartment, but this establishment is sort of my home away from home, for now. Did I tell you-" I said.

Abbot said, "Oooh! What did someone tell you? Something sweet and dirty?"

"…You think you could leave, Abbot?" I said.

"Sorry, no. I'm bored. Unless you'd care to wake me up with one deep thrust… hottie…" Abbot said, putting a hand on Luke's thigh.

Luke carefully removed the hand, as Abbot giggled.

I told Luke that the Madame thought I was some harbinger of the apocalypse, as Abbot listened to our conversation.

"…I mean, it makes sense. Right?" he said.

"Of course I didn't come here to destroy the Earth. I just got bored of Hell." I said.

"Yeah, I know, but I still wonder how you did it. You *are* half the Devil, and I've wondered about how you got here ever since I met you." Luke said.

"Well, you know, you just cross the river, go up the steps, and break through the eternally sealed stone portal. The portal was the hardest part for me, but there was an earthquake, or tremor, or something in

Hell, and a tiny crack opened up. I squeezed myself through, and it shut behind me." I said.

Luke said, "Sounds pretty easy, actually."

"It is incredibly difficult, I just summed it up neatly. I also had to sneak out of the house… with my dad, the Devil, and his dog, Cerberus, keeping me in. Charon wouldn't even let me cross the river, said it would break something if I got out, so I made a makeshift raft out of… well, corpses. If you touch the water you'll never come out, so it was hard even just paddling with that severed arm-" I said.

Abbot said, "You make me incredibly sick, Devil's Daughter. I think you completely turned me off. Come visit, hottie, and don't bring the girlfriend." and got up, winked at Luke, and disappeared.

"Alright. Where were we…" I said, putting a hand on Luke's thigh.

We had our awesome fun again, in our conjoined dreams, and actually waking up was very, very pleasant, after such a very, very pleasurable dream.

10

I was cleaning the house again, and I had flashes of the undead rooster in my mind.

Seeing through its eyes, escaping from the hounds in the forest that tried to rip it to pieces.

The rooster crossing the road, evading the cars. Why did it do that? Where was it going?

The rooster having chicken sex with a living hen. Was this an abomination, or just life?

But the rooster was dead, and continued to pick for bugs, to devour others' life.

It freaked out a few people who looked at it, them saying, "Oh mijn God... Ik denk dat er iets mis is met die kip."

The rooster cocked its head at the people, and the people ran away.

I had a strange feeling as it hid from animal catchers, fleeing them in the day.

The rooster wouldn't die so easily, because it was alive.

The Madame counseled me about this rooster. I was curious what I should do with it. Kill it? This seemed slightly like a mistake.

"Hmph. You could try to raise even more, if we get you some proper corpses. Would you like that? I am a little curious to see what Holland's last king would like to see of the country. Maybe we can treat him to our services?" the Madame said.

"I don't know… I have a craving for grain, now, because of that rooster in my head. I don't think I need a craving for women too." I said.

There was a fruit fly flying around in the room, and quickly, the Madame smashed it in clapped hands, wiped it off on a napkin, and gave the napkin to me.

"Here. Try and raise the fruit fly back to life." the Madame said.

"…But it's mostly just blood." I said.

"Try anyway." she said.

Ok… so… how do I find a fruit fly's soul in the afterlife? I looked at the dead corpse, mostly squished, and looked for it in the afterlife.

Do fruit flies even have souls? Do they go to Fruit Fly Heaven under Fruit Fly God?

I found the fruit fly, who was an angel fruit fly sitting on-

Sitting on a human angel's shoulder.

He offered me the fruit fly, and I trembled.

The gates of Heaven stood just behind him.

"Is it not this little guy's time?" the angel said.

"U-Um… the Madame wants me to bring him back." I said.

"Do you want to try at a second go, fruit fly?" the angel said.

The fruit fly buzzed into my hands.

The angel crossed his arms, and said, "Be wary of the souls you bring to life, for they will be your children, Mary Jane. Their suffering, their pain, will be your own."

"You're not going to stop me?" I asked.

"No. I am not going to fight you. It is not mine to take a life. You will realize that none have that strength, besides God." he said.

I opened my eyes, and looked down at the fly.

I gasped in terror.

It was buzzing, wriggling in its own blood, stuck to the napkin and squished.

The Madame said, "Interesting. Perhaps we can heal it-"

I squished the fruit fly to nothing, and I felt its pain, even the lingering pain as it was alive. It was... terrible.

Its soul buzzed back to Heaven, and I said to the Madame, "I don't ever want to do that again."

"Oh, did St. Peter hassle you at the gates? I always throw stones at him when I'm about to die, but he still doesn't let me in. Probably impossible to take more souls that go through there, with those giant pearly gates..." the Madame said.

I sighed, thanked her for the counseling, and snuck off to the pantry.

I devoured an entire bag of grain, just to get rid of this craving from the rooster.

I curiously, when the day was up and I was asleep, went to Heaven's gates again.

I waved to St. Peter, and the fruit fly, and asked St. Peter... very cautiously, if I could come in.

St. Peter opened the gates for me, as my heart was thumping.

"...It's that easy?" I asked.

"A visit is ok, occasionally, especially in a dream." St. Peter said.

I carefully snuck through the streets of happy, angelic houses, filled with happy, angelic people.

I saw too many fantastic things to ever explain, and they were all... welcoming. This was far unlike Hell, where everything seemed to push you away, or worse, cause you unimaginable suffering. Heaven was sort of like Earth, but unlike it in the way Earth was similar to Hell.

And I saw Him, waiting for me with open arms, calling me His daughter.

I ran to Him down the street.

And I wrapped my arms around Him in a gentle hug.

I then woke myself up.

And began crying in my bed.

God was always how I imagined him, like the father I always wanted… and he loved me too, and did the first thing I wanted from a real father… he hugged me gently.

I went out for a cigarette in the night, wearing my sweatpants.

It was still loud and bright, in the red light district, people laughing and partying in the streets.

I went to a coffee shop to smoke a bowl.

These places, coffee shops, were actually usually far from welcoming, especially in this city, filled with tourists. You bought overpriced weed, albeit good weed, and smoked with people grinning and glaring at each other, thinking they were living the life.

It had a strange sort of dark vibe to it… unlike just sitting back and smoking with your friends, in the coffee shops of this city. Almost criminal, even though it was technically legal to buy.

I smoked alone, and quickly decided to leave the coffee shop. I'm sure there were better ones, but this one was seedy, even with the cool, hip, luxurious setting.

I just sat by the water, like Luke and I used to do back home.

I thought of the Father who wished to claim me, if I wanted it.

I continued to smoke marijuana, and thought there was no one so blessed as me, Mary Jane-

But then I remembered I was the Devil's Daughter.

My father arose from the water, and did not offer his arms for a hug.

HE simply stared at me.

He knew I was his.

I walked away. Leave my dad be, and maybe if you're lucky he'll leave you be…

I kept telling myself this, as he followed me down the road.

I was soon running from the Devil, and got back inside the house, locking the doors with my maid keys.

I woke Abbot up, and asked her if we could pray.

She blinked at me sleepily, and said, "...Even though this is not the best time, as your artist and I were doing *such amazing* things together in my dreams... I will always take time to pray."

I ignored her comment, and we sat on her bed and prayed the rosary.

I knew the Devil was watching from the window, but I also knew he hated praying, so eventually left.

I sighed in relief, in the middle of a prayer, and began shaking.

I burst out crying from fear, and Abbot opened her eyes wide at me.

11

I jealously looked at Abbot, wielding only her fingers and making magical, sparkly rainbow fireworks flash from her pinky in this training session.

I wielded my princess wand, and shot out a fart from it. A literal fart. I was trying to do what she did...

Abbot laughed, and said, "Your talisman is trash, man. Literally. It was the only thing we could find for you."

"...What do you use? You don't seem to have a talisman." I said.

She brandished her hand with a ring on it, and said, "See this? This is my father's ecclesiastical ring. Gave it to me after he left the order. I *was* using my grandma's wedding brooch for so long... but this one seems a little stronger."

"A priest's ring? Oh. I've got one of those too." I said, brandishing my own ring.

"...Why do you have a sacred clerical object?" Abbot said.

"My boyfriend stole it for me." I said.

"...You're blasphemous." she said, and shot out a few snake illusions into the air which tied into knots, then turned into doves and flew away.

I tried to channel from the ring, but I don't know. I never took much heedence in its power, thinking it more like pretty stolen jewelry my boyfriend got me. It meant a lot to me, but it sure didn't seem magical. Seemed almost mundane, actually.

I waved the princess wand again, and tried to do what I was good at. I used fire.

Gosh... making fire from this thing sure smelled awful, like burning plastic... but I could, if I tried really hard, get it to come out in a condensed stream, rather than chaotically and wild like with my hand.

Malena used a knife, pricked her finger, and made blood droplets flow out into a heart around her.

"You're lucky, Malena." Abbot said, "You've got the best body, and the best work... I mean, I'd love to do that BDSM stuff, but they say I'm too harsh when I beat the shit out of them. I thought they liked that?"

Malena made the blood rain out of her finger, upward, and said, "You can't have pain without pleasure, pleasure without pain. BDSM stuff is really quite loving, in a different sort of way. If you aren't, you're not doing it right!"

Francesca just drew with her pencil, and made moving figures walk out of her portraits. I shook hands with myself in lead, before it poofed into nothing.

Tas smoked a cigarette, and watched. She said, "You all have such great magic... I don't really know how to do anything like you're doing."

"That's cuz you're a guy, Tas." Abbot said.

Tas blushed, and said, "...That is just the rudest thing I have ever heard."

"I'm joking. You're maybe just not as 'feminine' as us. I almost *do* think you're a guy, sometimes, when you're staring at my butt..." Abbot said, smirking.

Tas looked away from her, and said, "I think you all have great form, especially in magic, but you need to work on your conversation skills. There's a different sort of magic in a finely honed piece of literature, in dialogue and even in body language. You act as if you're all the most perfect alive, but I can see in your forms that it is a front.

"In conversations you must make every form of communication, you must be totally attuned to it without even trying at it, because if you're stiff they will tell. It's worked very handy for me, using just a good smile sometimes, when your life is on the line and all you've got is your language at your disposal."

I said, "Thanks for the tip, Tas. You always are the most welcoming of us and the most relaxed, with just a smile and nice words."

Tas smiled at me.

Francesca said, "This is very boring to me. I don't know why we're training these skills, when I could be crunching out more numbers. I think I can get a 1% increase in profits, if I work harder on this other 'front' of ours... Y'know that new brand of chips? The poofy ones? I'm going to rip them off, in just the right way, and open up another commercial side for the Madame."

Tas said, "Yeah. They have a great chip, but the advertising is complete crap. We could probably appeal to the kiddos, give 'em something savory and salty even though it's basically pork rinds."

Francesca said, "Exactly my thoughts. We're getting all this crap meat from the U.S. mass market, and pork has been taking a dive recently. Could line our pockets better, and give us a nice little vacation, maybe."

"...Um... How much do you all get paid? Do you get paid in more lessons?" I asked.

Abbot and Malena joked about the cash they were getting, saying that soon they could buy a mansion and a yacht if the Madame didn't take such a steep cut. Tas told us about this one drug deal making millions of euros she was proud of in the past, and Francesca smiled and said when it was my business to know, I would know.

I gulped. I was only being paid a maid's salary, and these girls were raking in the cash.

After our training session, I discussed my pay with the Madame. She said, "...Do you think you are not being paid adequately?"

"I was just, y'know, hoping to get more? I've been doing great work, everything is spotless-" I said.

She said, "You haven't taken out the chef's trash in a week. Maybe if you do more around the house, we can discuss this later..." and sighed.

"...But... I can't physically lift that giant bin." I said.

"You have magic for a reason, Mary. I suggest you try to use it... I *am* teaching you the applications of your power, so try and actually find a foothold in the lessons... You would've been paid more as a bartender, with tips too, but well... You burned it down." she said, "It's costing me a lot, just trying to hush up those now insane people you hurt, and to pay for the damages to the city. Mayhaps I should charge you, instead of pay you?"

I gulped, and said, "I'll clean out the bin." and left quickly.

Shit... I usually could finagle whatever I wanted out of my employers, but the Madame was a hardass. I looked at the bin, and decided... hmm... Guess I'll burn the trash. Nothing like cleansing fire.

12

"But it was a controlled flame! Nothing else got burned!" I said to the chef after he had doused the entire bin in what was going to be our dinner, the soup.

He wiped the sweat off his brow, and said, "I hate the flame. It hurts."

He could barely speak English, being a natural French man, and had these long burn marks all over his arms. Apparently he got into a cooking accident when he was younger, but I think that was just a rumor, the story about the flambé that fought back.

"You stay out of kitchen. It is sacré." he said.

"...But how am I going to clean the trash, then?" I said.

"You no burn. Stay out of kitchen." he said, with almost a desperate look in his eyes.

"...Is something wrong?" I asked.

He looked at the burns on his arms, and looked back at me, saying, "No. Please."

I left the kitchen.

We had dinner, all together, and for some strange reason... I really felt at home with these people. We laughed and joked, and got into great conversations about our previous homes. Most of the people here were from all sorts of places, coming together under the Madame.

The chef shakily placed the new soup in front of me, and quickly left. He looked kind of scared of me, for some reason.

I decided to catch him when he was taking a smoke and we had all finished dinner.

I started a smoke beside him, and he jumped and said, "Mon Dieu, comme dans mes rêves."

"What's that mean?" I asked.

"...Nothing. You are scary." he said.

"...Why? It's not like I did anything to you." I said.

"Your father is my god. And le Diable will take his due." he said, putting out the cigarette.

"...Oh! You're a satanist! Oh, that's cool. It's hard meeting anyone who gets where I came from-" I said.

"Non non non. I am ex. I was anarchist, satanist, adorateur du diable... I am ex." he said.

"...I see. Well, we can talk about it? Did you ever use the goat's blood orgy ritual?? That one's my favorite-" I said.

"I am ex... and non, I do not use goat's blood. The blood of the lives I have taken... will haunt my steps. The bridge burned, and with the bridge, me." he said, "I do not want to talk... but I must tell you, I will escape your father, mon Dieu-" he said.

"I hope I can, as well." I said.

"...Really?" he said.

"Yes. It's not good being chained to someone you don't like... especially if you're *supposed* to like them. My father kept me in the dark for so long, and made my human mother kill herself, I don't know how, but he did it and I am sure. I miss her, even though I never knew her, every day." I said.

"...I miss my wife. She burned with the bridge. I tried to go back for her, but it was too late." he said.

"Well, we all need to burn our bridges, every now and then." I said.

"Fourteen people died. Men, women, children. And my wife, who was pregnant." he said.

"...Oh. Well, I'm sure you'll be ok... I guess... Your soul will be fine! Yeah!" I said, doubting my words for his soul.

"My soul belongs to the Madame, and with her, ton Diable. I must clean..." he said, going back inside.

I said, "Allow me to help? I won't burn anything, I swear."

"...If you swear." he said.

"I swear I won't burn anything in the kitchen, by my mother." I said.

He smiled, and we cleaned up the dishes and things.

13

"Um… I know this is odd…" I said to Luke in a dream.

He frankly looked kind of frightened. Well, also kind of aroused, but that was the look I was going for.

"Er. We can try whatever you like! But what about the…" he said.

"Oh, I don't know, I was just curious… We don't have to. But maybe I can whip you? Just a little bit?" I said.

"…That's really what turns you on?" Luke said.

"Not… Not always. I just want to punish you, yeah, for seeing that nun behind my back… Stupid nun…" I said, stroking my whip.

He held my hand, as I put the whip aside in our dream dungeon.

"It wasn't an affair or anything. I just needed some extra support." Luke said.

"But- But wasn't it an affair? Even if you two weren't doing anything?" I said.

"…How so?" he said.

"God… Don't be stupid. You know you can have an affair, even without bodily pleasure. It's more- an affair of the heart… You were missing a woman, and you wanted to be with one, not even the bodily, sexual acts. Just to be with one." I said.

"I guess that's sort of true. But I think of Jone as just a friend, not a lover, and especially not as someone like you." Luke said.

"...I actually think of her as my best friend back home... I know that's weird for a demon chick like me to have a nun as a friend, but-" I said.

"I don't think that's weird at all." Luke said, "I won't pray with her anymore, if you don't want. Heck, I usually only ever pray by myself, and that's when the voices start up and I need a mantra. It was interesting praying with someone else."

"I can get that, and it's fine. I pray with a slut. You know, that one slut who intruded on us? That slut." I said.

"I'm glad you're making friends. We all need some more people, even just for support." Luke said.

"I didn't say she was my friend. She's the biggest bitch here." I said.

"...Well, you know, birds of a feather..." he said, grinning.

I pushed him, and laughed. "Don't make me actually have to punish you. You mean you don't find any of this... stuff... intriguing?"

"I like that bit, over there, but don't tell anyone." he said, pointing to an object on the side.

"Oooh. That's actually what I really like, too. Ok, get on the rack, our beautiful bed, because I'm going to love you... *hard.*" I said, picking up the object.

He grinned, as I began chaining him to the bed, and he said, "I don't have to call you a goddess, or something? To get in the role?"

"You can call me the filthiest slut." I said, making sure the chains were taught.

We smoked cigarettes after we were done, and got out of the dream dungeon to get some fresh air.

We went back to my rainbow skied forest, and enjoyed the many different dream entities that populated it. There were tigers drinking tea, frogs riding bicycles, and of course a lot of cheshire cats telling us jokes.

I sighed in happiness in the morning, after having such a nice dream. In a way, I was scared of that evil desire in my heart, stuff we did in the dungeon, but approaching it helped, and even sort of made it fluffy and gentle! What we did was at least not what happened in Hell.

I sighed in sadness as well, remembering Luke walk away into his own mind, with all those... *people...* yelling at him.

They weren't even people really, I hoped, but they sure made him suffer.

It's weird to think I was dating a schizophrenic, but it really made me happy. If anyone could understand my pain with the Devil in my own life, then it would be him, who fought against all sorts of evil creatures plaguing his mind. Luke was doing a lot better off, ever since I met him. It's one of the reasons why we're continuing the relationship.

But still... Those voices sure made me mad.

I took medicine, now, to stop against my own voices, the voice of my father. I took a pill every morning and night. Luke was lucky enough just to take an injection once a month.

I got to work, and cleaned up the stage, where I found the couple who performed the same act every night for the audience.

He said, "Diane... Really... Can't I have any more?"

"I'm sorry, Bob. But the Madame said if you take any more it will mess with your... performance." Diane said.

"B-But that only happened once!! I never meant for it to! You're very gorgeous, and I didn't mean not to be able to get it up-" Bob, the stupid idiot, said.

Diane said, "Are you sure you don't want to leave? I mentioned it once or twice. You can go back home, if you want."

Bob said, "No, I want to marry you, and have kids, and a nice home. We can do that, I swear."

"I'm sorry Bob. But I will never be pregnant with your child. I do not love you, and my home is here." Diane said.

Bob looked heartbroken.

He looked defeated.

And instead of crying, he pulled out a knife.

He tried to stab Diane… but of course, she was one of us.

When he stabbed her, he had only stabbed himself, in the heart.

Diane got up, walked to me calmly, and said, "Suicide… I think it's your job to clean that up, before the evening." and she walked away.

I sighed, and dragged the corpse outside.

I set it on fire, and then went back to clean up the blood.

Diane was rather a loner, not talking to any of us, ever. She only said something once or twice if she needed to, the rest of the time she was busy as a whore.

I realized she was cold, heartless, and when she said to Bob she didn't love him… that went for the rest of us too.

She had the scariest grasp of magic, as well. I couldn't really explain it, but when I confronted her for being so uncaring to Bob, when I ate my food, my food was eating me.

It was a terrifying sort of magic, not being able to understand what was even happening to yourself, and then you stab yourself hard with a knife, just trying to cut some steak.

I sat with the nurse, Diamond, for a second, as she healed my bleeding arm with a wave of a scalpel.

"This was the first surgery tool I ever used… I can't really use it for an actual surgery anymore, since it's so filthy, but it sure does bring back memories." Diamond said, showing off her talisman, the scalpel.

"It's beautiful. Like pure silver." I said.

"Oh, it's just common steel, but thank you. I hope you don't cut yourself anymore, since even though I find our conversations a delight, it would be pointless to have them with you bleeding out every day." she said.

"Ach, it was just Diane… I think. Was it?" I said.

"There are many different people here, and not all have your best interests in mind. I would tread carefully, lest they tread on you instead." Diamond said.

"Thanks. I hope you don't take this as offensive... but you seem far more experienced than us with magic, so I'm wondering why you're here at this school." I said.

"These girls need a helping hand, once or twice. It is actually a place I can naturally be myself as well... It was hell being expelled from medicine for my projects, and my appetites. Some will never understand the march of progress. Do you?" she said.

"...I'm not sure." I said.

She sighed, smiled in delight, and said, "Good. I'd hate for you to have to be my next subject... You look so tantalizing, and it would be a shame to ruin it. I also am very curious of your devil parts, and other parts as well. I believe you should think on the beautiful day, and try not to eat yourself anymore."

I smiled, shook her hand, and left back to my day.

I could feel her undressing me with her eyes as I walked away.

14

You really don't love me?

Shut up, wand. You're pink, sparkly, and plastic. You're for little girls.

...But I can be bigger, and stronger.

Goddamn, am I having this dream again? Are you trying to act phallical? You're a pink princess wand.

...Do you think you can make me bigger? I could be the biggest in the entire world-

I think you need to understand that I'm not going to masturbate with a princess wand.

I meant in strength. I can give you power, beauty, love. All things, if you believe in me.

God, just be quiet, I'm trying to dream of someone nicer than you. I was really going to have a few dream affairs myself, just to see how it felt.

...Could I be that person? I am magic.

Fuck it, go ahead, stupid wand.

The wand turned into a handsome, dashing man... who was rather short... wearing a fairy costume.

I looked down at him, and said, "Huh. I guess you're not as big as you expected, huh?"

"I can be taller. I can be handsomer. I can wear a suit."

I burst out laughing, and said, "Gosh... Ok. Whatever. Let's have tea, and I'll get this affair out of my heart... Haha..."

We chatted for a bit about the plastic he was made of.

"I'm actually made of polyethylene, the most commonly used plastic." he said.

"...So you're common. Weird and common." I said.

"I thought that would be attractive? Being made of the most durable, efficient piece of material?" he said.

"See, that's what you start with when trying to impress someone." I said.

He sipped at his tea, and said, **"Sorry. I am new to this sort of thing. The last person who held me was a little girl whose parents died in a fire."**

"...Oh. Kinda sad. What happened to her?" I asked.

"She grew up, and didn't need the strength of a princess wand anymore." he said.

"So why do you think I need your strength, huh?" I said.

"Because you were always the magical princess. You never thought you were, but it was always inside of you."

I wiped my slight tears out of my eyes, and said, "That's beautiful. I think that's actually what I needed."

"Now, hone your strength. Become the magical princess you always wanted, and make me bigger-" he said.

"I already told you. I don't want to sleep with you, and just was seeing what an affair of the heart is all about."

"I mean in strength. Take ahold, for you are magic." he said, and offered a hand.

I shrugged, and held his hand.

He turned into the plastic, sparkly wand, and I swished it around.

And in a way, I indulged this fantasy, and thought of myself as a princess. A magic princess, not a Devil's Daughter or even just a maid.

I swished my wand again, letting it sparkle, and it felt bigger.

I felt bigger, and stronger, and even magicaler.

I held the wand to the sky, and let it grow, becoming the most magic wand of all.

I was the princess of the world, the most magicalest, and my wand showed this to all.

It was the most beautiful piece of plastic in the world.

And while I was holding it above my head, the wand turned into the fairy guy again, and I collapsed under his weight.

"Oh. Sorry. I am your fairy godfather, and with my magic wand, you will always be a princess." he said, helping me back up.

"...I'm gonna ignore that comment, and just call you Chuck, ok?" I said.

Chuck shrugged, and poofed back onto my waist as a wand.

In the morning I worked on transmuting Chuck- my princess wand. I tried to change his form, make him bigger and stronger, but I didn't really know how to do that right.

Abbot said, "I would just use an illusion. It looks like crap, you might as well make it into something better, or at least look like something better, eh?"

Francesca said, "No, no... She needs to use her fire, slightly. It's obvious, you dummy. She wants it to *really* be stronger, and not just an act."

We stood outside of the house, and I used my fire slightly on the princess wand. I let my heat, my fire, course through the wand, and take ahold of the polyethylene, and change shape.

I turned it into a pink, sparkly dildo by accident.

Embarrassed, I hid it behind my back.

Abbot laughed, and said, "You know there are sex shops everywhere around us? You can just go buy a real one, instead of trying to make your own? They have lots of great toys. This one I got-"

Francesca gently took my hand back out from behind my back, and looked at the object. She said, "Not bad. A lot of girth. I mean, you *could* use this as a talisman, if it gives you strength. Have you ever heard of the British Bloody Bitch? She used a dildo, and massacred half the population of Britain with just her sex toy. She was an old medieval practitioner, and sex toys weren't looked favorably on at those times."

I quickly shot the heat through the... pink, sparkly, sex toy, and turned it into a sword.

It was magnificent, a shining piece of material, plastic albeit, but as I touched the tip I knew it was sharp, deadly, and strong.

Abbot said, "Now that's more like it. If you're gonna kill someone, may as well kill them with a sword. It's classy, and I'm sure the murdered appreciate being killed with such an outdated weapon. Can't it just be a gun?"

Francesca said, "Hmm... A plastic gun? Who ever heard of a plastic gun? I'm sure it's possible, but maybe you should use the element you're good at, and burn the dummy over there with your... princess thing."

I brought the princess sword back, and lunged it at the dummy from twenty feet away, and shot fire in a thrust with it.

The dummy roasted into flames, cut in half with pure fire and then burned to nothing.

I looked fondly at Chuck. *Now* I had a talisman.

And... when I was alone... I had an affair with him. A proper affair. Ahh...

He *was* just made of plastic, and I think I really needed to get that out of my system. I turned him back into a wand again, put him by bedside, and fell asleep to tell my boyfriend all about my naughty Chuck, who could take whatever shape I wanted.

Luke was actually kind of jealous of my dildo. I thought that was the appropriate response. I still kissed Luke before I woke up, and told him to pray with all his might with my nun, whenever he liked.

He kissed me, and then said he couldn't wait for me to come back home. It's what he was praying for.

I smiled as I woke up. Well! I couldn't wait to see him, too. He told me he was working on a few good pictures of me, said he saw them in his mind's eye.

I hummed as I worked, thinking of what naughty, erotic, beautiful poses he imagined me doing. Really I was just taking out the garbage, but it's nice thinking that someone else is thinking of you that way.

15

Tas asked me to help her on a job. "I just need a pretty face. These guys expect a cool, lesbian couple, so I need some arm candy."

"...Really? What kind of people are they?" I asked.

"Gangbangers from the Middle East. They've sunk their hooks into some of our businesses, and if I don't get them *out* of my hair, then they'll bring all their buddies to muck things up too..." she said, smoking a cigarette beside me outside of the house.

"So what are you going to do about it?" I asked.

"Well, I was thinking of killing them, actually, but they're from some hogwash royalty. I'm just going to politely tell them to back off." she said, "So will you help me?"

"Sure. Sounds fun. I'll wear my nice clothes-" I said.

"Excellent. Meet you at the hash house down the road in an hour, ok?" she said.

"...In an hour?" I said.

"Time's a wasting! I'll repay you somehow." Tas said, kissed me on the cheek, and left to vanish down the alley into the city.

I got clothed in... hmm... I guess I'd wear the skirt. It was a little revealing, but was something that I got for free from the house.

I met Tas at the hash house, with two middle easterners laughing and joking with her in their native language.

I think if those guys could they would jam their eyes up my skirt, their gaze was so heavy.

Tas kissed me long, and I knew by her body language I needed to play this part, so kissed her back. There was a slight aura of... fear, in her embrace.

I sat beside Tas, and one of them switched up their language for my benefit.

The tall, very bearded man said to Tas, "I am so glad to meet someone from our home. You are one of the few who's actually from our homeland, and it is so pleasant to meet such a familiar accent. Your father was a soldier, correct?"

Tas said, "Yes. He was one of the invaders, but was quickly conquered by the land itself."

The big bearded man laughed and said, as the other was silent, "Conquered by our beautiful women, you mean. As I see you have by these Dutch girls! Ha ha!"

"Oh, she's an American. Say Hello, Mary. This is Sahib and Khaled." Tas said. I waved to them.

"Now, to get into business..." the big bearded man, Sahib, said, then switched to his native language again, but Tas stopped him.

Tas said, "I think you should let the merchandise speak for herself. It is a big thing, to give up someone's home for a far away land."

Sahib looked at Tas, then back at me, and said, "I will take you for five thousand euros."

The blood was draining in my face, and I was wondering if I really could trust Tas.

Tas was outraged, and said, "Five thousand euros?? A woman is a thing of beauty, and you want to give me five thousand euros?? I will take five million euros, or you can ship off without her."

"Can she... perform under pressure?" Sahib said.

"She can perform with both hands bound behind her back and with a banana shoved up her ass." Tas said.

Sahib relayed this to Khaled, and Khaled grinned, and nodded.

"Done. We will pick her up tomorrow-" Sahib said.

But Tas said, "And I want one more thing...

"I offer my proposal of marriage to you, Khaled, from the Madame. We will conjoin our forces! Take the world by storm. Together, we shall-" Tas said.

Sahib quickly told Khaled, and they were both taken aback, and Sahib said, "...Is this a joke?"

"For one so great as yourself, I think you should accept this proposal, or risk our deal." Tas said, arms crossed.

Khaled said something in his native language forcefully, and Sahib said, "You are a filthy slut! A blasphemy to us! No woman has this right, especially not one who loves its own."

Tas said, "Very well... I meant a marriage of operations only. I never meant a marriage in bed. But very well. If you do not find our women satisfactory, you insult the Madame, and our trust. The deal is off, and I *assure you...* You won't find another seller, at least in this city."

Sahib relayed to Khaled, and Khaled rubbed his eyes. He spoke to Tas again in their native tongue, and Tas and him shook hands, and the two left.

Tas breathed out a sigh of relief when they left.

"...Were you really going to sell me? Or was that a trick?" I asked.

"A lie. I was seeing how far they wanted to get into bed with us, and I knew they didn't want the full package. I was really hoping to play on their pride... Honor means a lot in the Middle East, and them insulting ours gave us a quick way to shove them aside." Tas said.

"So you being from the Middle East was a lie, too? I thought you were from Holland? Where are you from, really?" I asked.

"No, that was partly true. My father was a soldier… and we travelled a lot. I think I can call myself from Holland, though, living here for so long." Tas said, "Well! Wanna get a beer? My treat."

"Sure. But you owe me more than a beer, but I'll think of something later." I said as we left the hash house.

We drank a lot, and she didn't flirt with me, she didn't make any unwanted advances. I had made myself clear to her earlier, and she respected my position and stance.

It's too bad for those thugs that they didn't respect ours… I asked Tas if there will be more, and she said, "There will always be more like that, from all over the world. Best we can do is delay them, if we can't fight them all. Gang wars are no fun." Tas told me all about sex traffickers, slavers in actuality, and said she despised their very smell. "Ever since I saw one of their victims… a child, who was taken by this one gang, I began working under the Madame. Her position is clear against people like that, and we make a point to give old sex slaves homes, real homes they can be proud of, and not be raped as they're crying in fear."

"…But the Madame owns one of the most popular brothels here…" I said.

"And don't you forget it. She is the Madame, and sometimes it is hard for old dogs, or old whores, to learn new tricks. Here at least they're safe, and we teach them ways they can protect themselves far over giving them a gun, like I learned how to do. Don't tell anyone this… but Diane is one of the people like that, a child sex slave. Now… she holds all the power in relationships. When she fucks with you, you're basically fucking yourself." Tas said.

"I'll keep that in mind, and won't fuck with her, then." I said.

"Good. Stay safe, Mary. You need anything else? I hate a debt that I can't get off my back…" she said.

"I want you to ask your Belgian girl out. For me. I think you're a great person here, and heck, if I wasn't in such a good relationship, I might take a gander at being a real lesbian couple with you." I said, smiling.

She grinned, and said, "Maybe someday. If she wasn't like you, and in 'such a good relationship' then I'd have taken off with her around the world by now. Maybe you'll change your mind about me in a few years."

I said, "Oh, no, I think I could get off with you in a flash-"

"No. I mean you'll think differently of me. Stay safe, Mary Jane, because not everyone is the good guy, no matter how often we like to play the part." Tas said, smiled, and paid for our beers, and left me alone at the bar.

16

I saw that rooster staring at me from across the street. It looked like he wanted me to come over.

I ignored it, cleaned up the rest of the house... then went back to peek out the window.

It was still staring at me from across the street.

I guess I'd meet it? I went outside, looked at the rooster, and crossed the road to meet it.

I looked down at it, and it stared up at me continuously. Its eyes were gone, rotted out.

It really looked like a monstrosity, actually, but I saw myself through its eye sockets looking at me.

I followed it down an alley, as it seemed to want to show me something.

I blinked. There was a dog mauled to pieces.

I gasped, as I looked at something by the dumpster. There was an animal catcher, dead.

I saw what it had done, in my mind's eye.

It had mauled a dog to bits, after the dog finally caught it.

It had ripped the animal catcher's throat out with its talons, after the catcher finally caught it.

I lit the corpses on fire, and was going to roast the rooster too.

But the rooster escaped, as the other corpses burned to nothing, bones collapsing in ashes.

Shit! I chased the rooster, and I was nearly going to catch it-

Shit. I knew what happened when you caught the rooster.

It flew at me, scratching at my jugular with its talons, pecking at my eyes as I shielded my face.

I tried to scorch it, but I couldn't see under its relentless onslaught.

I felt its pain, for attacking its mother, who only wanted me to be proud of it.

I cried in fear, as I was on the ground, shielding my vitals from the rooster's fury.

There was no one to save me but a few tourists who yelled at the rooster and screamed at it, trying to kick it away. The rooster ran off down the alley, and the tourists helped me up.

They were a few Americans, a couple abroad, and they asked me if I was alright. The woman looked kind of like a hippie, with long armpit hair, and the guy was thin and tall, who was recording this scene with his phone.

They offered to take me to a hospital, saying that that rooster looked diseased or something, but I said no, no, I just needed to go home.

They insisted, saying that a working girl like me shouldn't be harassed.

I said no, no, I just needed to go home.

They demanded me to go with them, saying they were going to call an ambulance for me.

I looked into their eyes. I looked at what they had been doing in the red light district.

They were having a very relaxed vacation, threeways every second with the prostitutes, and they were genuinely frightened for me.

They made me sick.

I yelled, *"If you don't let me go home right now, I will report you for harassment to the police. Get your hands off of me."*

They let go of me, after they were trying to drag me to the hospital.

I huffed in anger when I got back home. Stupid rooster, and stupid tourists. Both of them should just mind their own business, and realize when someone doesn't want their help, they should back off. Well, I don't know how the rooster was trying to help me, but it seemed like it wanted *something* from me.

I hoped it didn't kill any more people. I had finished my duties in the house, so went to a lesson the Madame was giving.

17

Abbot said from beside me, "...You ok, Devil Girl? You look like someone slashed you with their nails. You get in a bitch fight to defend your territory?"

"...A rooster attacked me." I said.

Abbot laughed, and said, "Gosh, you're weak. A *rooster??* Shit... Weak."

The Madame looked at me for a second, as I was all scratched up and bloody, then turned to the rest of the class and said, "You all need to learn how to defend yourself from the modern eye. Many of you are very powerful, specializing in dangerous powers, like fire or disorientation. To me, you are all strong and willful soldiers, that bow to none. To the public we are freaks.

"I want to show you something that has just become viral in the media."

The Madame turned on the TV, and showed the news, where they showed me getting beaten up by the undead rooster... and trying to light it on fire with my bare hands. The tourists had recorded this part...

I was red in embarrassment, as the class mumbled and talked amongst themselves.

They quieted down as the Madame said, "Many think this is a hoax, or a stunt, but it will catch a few people's eyes. I will show you a quick... erasure of this file."

The Madame waved her hands, and as the reporters were starting to talk about the reality of witches, they suddenly started talking about how cute kitty cats were, and the footage changed into one of an animal shelter.

"This is an international broadcast, and now your blunder, Mary, never existed but to a few.

"I didn't change the footage, I simply changed what your eyes see. The actual copy is still how it is, although has just been deleted by most since it's so incredibly boring. We live in a throw away culture, and this magic works very well for the dumb masses, who forget what they see as soon as it is out of view.

"Of course I had to tamper with a *few* memories of powerful figures... but only children, the insane, and the unimportant will remember this story, and spout conspiracy theories for times on after. I will show you how to change what others see. Please, discuss with your partner how you would hide your power." the Madame said.

Abbot and I turned to each other, and she said, "So you think you can make yourself popular, Devil Girl, by getting beaten up by a rooster? I wish I had an illusion for *anything* to make you more appealing..."

"Um... It only got into the news because it got popular... It could be any sort of thing with digital enhancement, so it's not that big a deal..." I said.

"Right... And when you try to get in the next spotlight, we'll be there before you try to be a Jesus we don't want... Poof! You'll pull out your powers, and then you'll just be a dogfucker, and no one will care..." Abbot said.

"...Is that what happened to you?" I asked.

"Nah. I just like to mess with people. They really think I'm the worst, and they get a kick out of it, in the lower regions, watching me degrade myself. Really they're the monsters, and by watching my degradation, they are only degrading themselves." Abbot said.

"...I guess that's true... I have felt shame seeing some things... especially things you do." I said.

"Only because secretly you enjoy it! Now, I've got a good knack for this sort of stuff, but I'm wondering how you would 'allude' to me that you're someone I should actually help..." Abbot said.

"I've got blood streaming down my neck. The reality doesn't appeal to you to help me? That's what those tourists *tried* to do, in their pushy way." I said.

"Nah. Just tells me you need to take a bath. Like, think of it like this... I'm a potential customer, and you're my whore. Why should I pay you to give me an ejaculation, hm? Why should I pay you for the full price, maybe even hooked a few more days and squeezing out my bank account for you? What would you do to please me?" she said.

"Have sex with you?" I said.

"...Boooring. I can make myself cum with one good hand. And you're already giving it all away! Nothing is free, Mary." Abbot said.

"...How is this a way to hide my power?" I said.

"What power? Power is an illusion itself." she said, and smirked.

"...Oh! So... I guess I would... *Talk like this?*

"I would show my true power, and have you doubt it.

"I would show the Devil's Daughter in me, let you wonder... and then I would-

"Just be me for a while. The me I show you. I'm the Devil's Daughter, Abbot, and you've been had ever since I met you.

"I'm the worst, and you think you're even worse than me. I've seduced you into Hell, with just your own disbelief in yourself.

"Your sins will always haunt you, and I will be there for you down below." I said.

I could practically see the goosebumps stand up on her.

She laughed nervously, and wagged a finger at me, saying, "...You *are* good! I didn't know you could do that thing with your voice! It's, like, not even magic! But it sure makes me shiver..."

I smiled, and briefly showed my fangs for a second. Abbot eeped.

The Madame clapped me on the shoulder, and made me jump.

The Madame said, "That is wise, Mary, to have people doubt your existence with true strength. Some don't even believe in the wrath of God... but as one who has felt it, seen it first hand, I can say with full certainty it does not feel good to be crucified. Would you like to hang up on the cross as well for showing strength to weaklings?"

I looked up at her, and said, "...But we could take those weaklings no matter what we do. What's the point of hiding, anyway?"

"Because we are all weak alone. Together we are strong. That is why you are all here, to find your strength... together. There are many more than us, and we are a very slim minority. We could be crushed if we are not wily and slippery like a snake." she said, removing her hand.

Abbot said, "...So... Tell me, why should I pay you? I certainly don't want to sleep with you *now,* now that you want to destroy my soul..."

The Madame walked away to another pair, and I said, "...I guess because I'm actually nice at heart, have a good life, and want you apart of it too..."

"Aww! See, that's why people want to sleep with you. Not because you're evil incarnate. When you bed with the masses, you become the masses, and are apart of their strength as well." Abbot said, smiling.

I looked back at the broadcast, and I was in it, but not using fire. I was cuddling a kitty cat.

I sighed, and smiled. It *is* safer being with the rest, no matter how estranged you feel. I guess the seduction is really in kindness, true kindness, and not fear.

The Madame said as much, and said that kindness comes with a price. It is a bargain of power, kindness for kindness. "We remember far more of danger than simple acts of goodwill, so take kindness into effect next time you need to cast an illusion or snip someone's memory." the Madame said, smiling kindly.

18

Luke and I chatted in a comfortable coffee shop in our dreams, where we first had coffee in real life, with cuddly cats serving us coffee.

"Wow! I feel so nice right now. This is like the best dream I've ever had!" Luke said, as we sipped coffee together.

I smiled, and said, "Even over our sexy dreams?"

"Well, those are a different sort of nice. This is just- I feel so relaxed." Luke said.

I sipped my coffee, and said, "Thanks. I'm trying to make up for being so nasty in the dungeon. I mean, I could've stopped when you said the safe word, but still… it did get you off."

"…Well, yeah, it was… hot! No holds barred, that kind of thing. I would really like it if you paid more heedence to that stuff in the future, however… I only felt safe even after I said it because I knew it was you." Luke said.

"So you really trust me? Why? I had it out for you even if I was being nice, when we first met." I said.

"Hm. Why shouldn't I trust you? Would you give me a reason to not?" Luke said.

"Hm. I guess not. You're right, I accept your trust, and place my trust in you as well. I mean, you could also have fought back, thrown in some of your craziness of your own mind. I've been in your madness once or twice, experienced what you felt… and I didn't enjoy it." I said.

"As I have yours. I feel like you are relatable to me, in a sense, even if we go through different madnesses." Luke said, and picked up a cat and cuddled it.

The cat mewled, and I pet him as Luke placed him on the table before me. Stupid cat. I don't know why I loved them so much now. At first I just thought they were dumb, snarky smartasses who laze around and puke up their own fur… but they've grown on me.

The cat said, "Oh, you've grown on us, too, Jane. We wouldn't all be here if you weren't such a welcoming individual."

"Am I too soft, though? I got beaten up by a rooster. Shouldn't I have torn it apart without mercy?" I said to Luke, as the cat jumped off the table.

"So why did you show it mercy?" Luke asked, "Roosters are territorial creatures, and not one to back down. It would've been safer if you broke its neck or something, albeit kind of harsh because it's just a rooster."

"This isn't just a rooster. It's a monster rooster that won't even die, since I brought it back to life. I guess I did feel kind of bad for it… Poor guy is just trying to live his life, even if he killed a few times." I said, sipping my coffee.

"…A killer undead rooster? Sounds like a bad horror movie." Luke said.

"I'm sure it's been done before. But yeah, I guess I should just find it and kill it for good." I said.

"…Maybe you can reason with it?" Luke said.

I shook my head, and said, "It's got a taste for blood now. I see it in my mind's eye, chasing people away just for the malevolence of it. It's got a name in the media now too, De Dodelijke Kip."

"…The Deadly Chicken… Huh. Kind of a double entendre. Chickens, or cowards, aren't supposed to be deadly, but this one is. And also an actual chicken." Luke said.

I laughed, and said, "I think the cowards are the scariest. You know they're hiding something, some true power after they've been pushed around too much."

Luke smiled, and said, "Nah. They just want to live their life. It's probably safer being a chicken, than a lion. Lions are hyped up as courageous, fearless, bold. But they get poached and killed all the time, nearly endangered. Chickens are probably the most common birds on the planet."

"That's true. I guess the cowardly lion must've done something right before he got his courage. Fucker lived to middle age, in cowardly retirement, before stupid Dorothy brought him on a suicide mission against the witch. I'm sure in the unedited version he gets shot by a few spells, standing up to the badass wicked witch, and meets his untimely demise." I said.

"But that's why people remember him! Better to live as a coward and then die a hero, right? That way you get the best of both worlds." Luke said.

I smiled, and said, "Feel like going to the dungeon for a bit?"

Luke shrugged, and said, "I trust you."

I took him to the dungeon, after I had dream redecorated, and it was just like our apartment back home. Luke gasped, as I made every nice thing especially nice just for him, and he said, "...This is no dungeon."

"It's my home, and I'm glad I can share it with someone as nice as you. Now ravish me. I expect to be saying the safe word a few times myself." I said, taking off my clothes.

19

The nurse, Diamond, was going to teach us bodily magic next.

Malena was great at this kind of stuff, often using it in her work to inflict pain or pleasure ten times more stimulating, and was Diamond's aide during this lesson.

Diamond had to stop Abbot from trying to cut Francesca open and then try to heal her back from pieces, so Malena was teaching Diane and I.

Diane was silent, as Malena said, "Now, we should really try something on your horns... I mean, it's not like they're not fashionable, but they do show off a little too much of the supernatural sometimes, y'know? Could scare someone who sees them by accident, or they may even get the wrong idea of your job!"

I said, "That's a good point. Some people think I'm cosplaying, or trying to play as a sexy demon chick. I *am* a sexy demon chick."

Malena giggled, and said, "And that you are! Do you remember how you poofed them out of your head? Is it anything like this?"

Malena chopped off a finger with her talisman, the knife, and I gasped as blood spurted out.

She calmly picked up the finger, and shot out a new finger from the stump.

"Now, that was a little bit of an extreme example, as it takes a lot of matter to restructure a whole digit like that. It's worked a couple times... er hem... with men who like things... tortured. Sometimes I've made mistakes, and had to resew their whole digit back on, then snip their memory so they think they had a good time! Gosh... the crying you get from grown men when they see their penis fallen off..." Malena said, shaking her head, "I want you to try to do the opposite of this, and absorb the matter back into your head."

"How the heck do I do that? They're horns. Should I just try to cut them off? They *did* fall off naturally when I had them the first time." I said.

"Nah. I think it will be helpful if you can retract them at will. Could come in handy? Like this." Malena said, and sculpted her body with a wave of her knife, reforming her breasts and feminine features... into that of a man's.

"Wow. That's... really something! You've got the whole package! And I mean a package!" I said, looking below her waist.

"Oh, it doesn't really work, and is just a coverup, but just the idea of it can do wonders. You know 'Sinbad,' right? Well. You're looking at him." Malena said.

I blinked, and then it clicked, "Oh! The blue light worker! Yeah, I saw you a few times. Gosh! I thought you looked familiar, but couldn't place from where."

Diane said, "Sinbad is great on stage."

"Sinbad" said, "You got that right, hun! Before we had that one guy, what's his name... Where did he go, now that I mention it? Whatever, before we had him, Diane and I would put on astounding performances all the time. The audience couldn't even tell the fake moans from the real ones! I think Diane really had a part to play in that, showing them what they wanted to see."

Diane smiled.

"Ok… So, how do I do that?" I asked.

Diamond had finished healing Francesca from pieces, and came over to us as Malena waved her over. Diamond said, "It all comes down to biology, chemistry, and the basic building blocks of life. You don't have to know *everything* about anatomy to do this, although it comes in handy… All you really need to know is how you want your body to feel, to look, and act under your pressure, and it will restructure itself to that will. To make it simple for the layman, look inside yourself and feel who you want to be."

"Hmm…" I hmmed, "Ok, I'll try to see how I see myself."

I closed my eyes, and saw myself with Luke, like him a human, as I saw myself in the mirror, sometimes how Luke drew me-

But there was an intrusive thought in my head I couldn't get rid of.

It was who I was before.

I couldn't shut out this image, and I just wanted to smash it to pieces like a twisted mirror at a carnival.

I wanted to destroy this piece of me.

But it only grew stronger, and stronger, until-

Malena screamed.

I opened my eyes, and said, *"What the fuck are you screaming about?"*

Diane jumped out of her seat and stepped back, and Diamond sighed and got me a mirror.

I screamed in anger, as I saw myself, the Devil's Daughter.

Red skin, red hair, red eyes, horns, fangs, bat wings on my back, my demon tail… and the hooves.

Blast this evil form!! Damn it to HELL!! DAMN YOU ALL TO HELL!!

I screamed, and flew out the window, like the monster I was.

I sat on the church roof long into the night, like a damn gargoyle… crying.

I was always this in the end, I was always this, and my brief change was just that, a brief change, a rest before my inner self came out again.

Well damn them all. I'll let them all see the monster, I won't hide anymore-

"We've all felt like the monster before." someone said.

I looked around.

No one was there.

"Who's there?? I'll burn this entire area if you don't show yourself-" I said.

"This is a voice in your head, Jane. Fuck, I've been hearing you for a while, actually, so I thought I'd respond. Is it freaky hearing your lover in your head? I know I thought so. A little disturbing, honestly." *the voice, one of the voices, said.*

"You know this is a trick. You haven't been taking your meds, Jane... You haven't been listening to me." another voice said.

"Oh, just leave her be. If you need to, come talk to me instead, Jane." *the other voice said.*

"You should really take your medication, Jane. Why haven't you?" the other voice said.

I screamed out, "I thought I was getting better! I thought I didn't need it anymore, because I had magic anyway! I'll blast you both if you don't shut up!!"

"I'm here for you, Jane."

"I'm here for you, Jane."

I started crying again... One was Luke, the other was Lucifer. Why couldn't I just have Luke, and not the other?

"Here, listen to a song, Jane. Most of my voices aren't very musical, but I can be. It's your magic doing this-"

"That's crazy! No one has that power! She's just hearing voices, like the lunatic that she is!"

"...Just listen to the song."

I sniffled, and heard the music. This sweet, sweet song that I heard only a few times, and forgot about again. This sweet, sweet song, always with me, that always came out during the worst.

I kinda... felt like dancing.

"Go for it, Jane. Music helps drown everything out, just don't fall off the roof."

I laughed, and danced to the sweet song, dancing on the roof and then flapping around in circles around the steeple, going straight up to the cross... and balancing on the very tip.

Luke had told me he always wanted to do that, y'know, if it was possible, and not fall off at such a great height.

I smiled, and I felt the breeze through my hair. I felt like my normal, human self. Me.

And the other voice said abruptly, *"Don't trip."*

And I tripped.

I fell down and down, and my wings had disappeared.

I fell to my doom. I wondered which place I would go to, as I fell.

And before I splat, I realized *I had strength.*

I had both. I was the demon, and loved.

I laughed at this thought, so magnificently. I could have both.

I flapped my wings out of my back, and soared again before hitting the ground, swooping away from the asphalt and scaring a rival brothel worker.

Snip, snip, goes her memories, she only saw me as a kindly dove when she looked again.

I flew back home, and landed at the back.

I sighed, put my wings back in, and rushed to the bathroom. I sighed in relief as I looked in the mirror, I was myself.

And if I looked just right... *I saw my other self.*

I laughed maniacally, and told Luke we would have the times of our lives as we soared together-

He said, "Take your meds, Jane. It will help, and this feeling will pass."

I stopped laughing, and nodded sadly.

I took my meds, and tried to drown out the voices of the two people in my head, my father, the Devil, and my boyfriend, Luke, as they got into an argument about me.

I hid under my bed sheets, and just tried to remember the music.

I realized this was another episode, and it would pass, as I fell asleep…

20

"Stupid Abbot... My skin itches everywhere I had to regrow it... Anyway, are you ok, Mary? You look a little odd." Francesca said in her office.

"Um... It just takes a while for the meds to work properly, although I feel a bit better now that I'm taking them again." I said.

"Hey, it's ok. It's hard to find anyone who doesn't have some sort of mental illness, from anxiety to schizophrenia, there's all sorts. I take a THC gummy every now and then. So what do you think of the chips?" Francesca said.

I had another of her spicy, salty, snack chips, which were basically pork rinds, and said, "They do taste... interesting. How did pork rinds even become chips, anyway?"

"You hate them... Shit. Did I use too much seasoning?" Francesca said.

I shrugged, and said, "It's not like pork rinds are *bad,* per say. My artist said they were the best thing he ate when he was in jail. But y'know, he was in jail, and didn't have any other good treat in there at all."

"...Do I use less pork? More corn flour?" Francesca said.

"I thought it was just pigskin? You use that?" I said.

"...I'm not certain. I was trying to use less skin to save a euro or two." she said.

"See, that's all well and fine, being efficient, but I think people will be able to tell that you're cutting corners with their food. If you don't give them something deliciously prepared, with all your heart, it will come out flat, sort of like these chips. They're supposed to be *fluffy* damnit! But it's ok. Really not bad for a stoned snack." I said, crunching on another pork rind.

"...In numbers that's all I do, cut corners. That's the way to save time and money. If I try to put my 'heart' into something, we'd be losing our jobs." she said.

I shrugged, and said, "It's a different sort of work. That's why those fast food places all make crap burgers, because they cater to mass consumption and cut corners everywhere they can. You should come to some places in America with me. There are the best burgers in the world, and they're just unknown, local mom and pop places who put real heart into their food."

"...So you're saying I should make it out of pig heart?" Francesca said.

"...Do you think that will taste good to you? I mean, I'd try it, maybe, but you should make something that you yourself will want to eat." I said.

"...They do make this dish in Britain with pig heart... Most people think our food is really weird, but I kind of like it. We know how to make fish and chips, I'll say that, but pork rinds? It's some crazy American scheme, and I can't wrap my head around it, and worse I'm stuck with these tons of pork skins from the U.S.!" Francesca said.

"I'm sure you'll figure something out. Experiment with cooking, just try whatever you like a few times. It's the experimentation which is fun." I said.

"...Ok. I'll look up some recipes tonight, and ask the chef about it... He should know, even if he's so *very* French." Francesca said.

"Want me to ask him? We've kinda bonded, and he's been teaching me some of his cooking skills in the kitchen." I said, putting the chips back on the desk.

"...You know he was a bomber, right? Escaped the law, somehow, maybe a guardian devil at his back. I secretly think it was the Madame the whole time." Francesca said, putting the chips in a drawer.

"I know. But we've all been bad people, at some point of our life. Really, I'm just trying to get his recipe for the steak. *Never* have I had such a good steak, even in America." I said.

"...You just cook it hot, right? Simple." Francesca said.

"Well, yes, but you've got to cook it all the way, through and through and not burn it, just rare enough. It honestly looks like he's dancing with the Devil, the way he makes the steak, making the heat just right." I said.

Francesca smiled, and said, "You put up a good American vibe, but it's weird thinking that you're a foreigner, from not even the *Earth*. From bloody Hell itself."

"Well, I'm at least half American, on my mom's half, and half Hellish from my dad. I came out of Hell in America specifically to look for my mom, and then kill her, and maybe seduce a few souls to evil if I had time, but then I met my artist, and things started looking even better than Hell." I said.

"...So it is genuinely nice with this person back home? What's it like?" Francesca said.

"Well, we've been getting together in our dreams, and that's been really awesome, but he didn't remember absolutely *everything* that happened until he started writing the dreams down. He's getting a lot better at details, now." I said.

"...Hm. I'd say you shouldn't do that, get together in dreams, because we don't have phones for a reason. It's to keep us focused on our-" Francesca said.

"Focused on what? Fucking, cleaning, and the books like you're doing? It doesn't need to be a prison, and I feel trapped without my phone." I said.

"A common feeling. But you've found ways to bypass barriers even without it. If you were dependent on technology, who knows how inhibited you'd be? You'd just be another pig, consuming cheap pork rinds, not able to leave your phone." Francesca said.

"I guess that is a good point. I got kind of hooked on technology, since if Hell has technology, you don't want it. It's a breather having everything available at the push of a button." I said.

"...So... About this artist... What's he do for you?" Francesca asked, blushing.

I opened my eyes wide, then grinned, and said, "Oh, he does this great thing when he kisses my neck-"

"I didn't mean sexually. I meant... like what's he *do* for you? Does he make you feel good, better, somehow? How?" she said.

I blinked. I said, "...Y'know, just be a good friend, be supportive, fight the Devil with me, shit like that. He's just someone I can depend on when things get bad for me. He wasn't always like that, but being together has helped us grow more together as individuals."

"...I see... He doesn't even check your work for you? Like a business partner, or maybe even a good mentor?" she said.

"Is that what *you* want from someone?" I asked.

"...Kinda. Someone I can go into business with, in realms of the heart. I imagine such a thing would really make me feel... complete. I've really just been having sex outside the house, with a... Never mind. That's none of your business. Anyway, I should get back to my own business, and I've kept you from your work for long enough. See ya, Mary Jane." Francesca said, straightening some pencils.

"See ya! Work on the rinds! Think if you were making them for that special someone, and I'm sure they'll be delicious!" I said, smiled, and waved at her as I left the office.

She smiled and waved back.

21

"She has sex with a dummy." Abbot said, smoking a cigarette on her bed, as I was cleaning our shared sleeping room and she had intruded in my mind and read my thoughts, and I was thinking about who Francesca was seeing.

"...I wish you wouldn't do that. If you do that again I'll-" I said.

"I know, I know, turn into a demon and terrorize me... It's just easier now. Your thoughts are so... *loud.* Those pills must've been helping you deal with crap like me." Abbot said.

"...I hate getting back on the regimen, but I know it will help. Sometimes I have mania, and then the depression, in between the voices... Just mini episodes, however. And what's wrong with having sex with someone not very smart?" I said, "Sometimes they think less, and please more."

Abbot rolled her eyes, and said, "We both know that's just a power play, where you can feel superior over your partner. But I meant an actual *dummy.*"

"...Like what? Pinocchio or something?" I said.

Abbot smirked, and said, "Instead of his nose growing... y'know. She's *great* with artsy stuff... It doesn't show on the surface, but she's really a magician with that pencil. The sex doll thing kinda freaks me out, though."

84

"...Is that healthy for her?" I said.

"Beats me. *You* named your dildo Chuck. What's the harm?" Abbot said.

"My Chuck is just an extremely magical talisman, that-" I said.

"That you get off with when we're all busy at mealtime. You're gonna starve yourself if all you do is try to orgasm instead of feed yourself." Abbot said.

"...I've been sneaking grain from the pantry... My undead chicken is giving me more and more cravings. I ate a fly the other day, and I enjoyed it." I said, embarrassed.

Abbot laughed, and said, "Gosh. You *are* the nutjob here. But actually, compared to when I first met you, I find that comforting. What at first would irritate and annoy me, now I just chalk up to your weirdness."

"...Thanks. Did we become friends, or something? I really, seriously, hate you sometimes." I said.

"And you as well, Devil Girl. But I suppose we could've picked worse 'friends.' Let's go get a drink, and some food, and some weed. I am just *starving* from this busy night, and want some inhibitors to dull my memories of it." Abbot said, getting up from bed and putting out the cigarette.

"I've still got to finish this room, and then I can-" I said.

"Screw it! It looks good enough, and I'll cover for you. C'mon, let's go." Abbot said.

I got dressed in some casual clothes, undressing as Abbot watched.

"You never told me about your tattoos before, Devil Girl. You've got one cross above your breasts... and then another upside down cross by your twat. What's the deal with that?"

I pulled up my pants, covering the tattoo again, and said, "The lower one was sort of... It's disgusting. It basically means that the lower part is for Satan."

"Oh. That is disgusting, yeah." Abbot said.

"He never- I mean, I'm not sure- But I- It was a weird time in my life..." I said.

"I never knew you *also* had daddy issues. Makes a lot of sense, actually." Abbot said.

"The top one is a breaking of the seal my dad put on me, and covers an invisible pentagram that used to flare up, which showed his power over me. I got the Christian cross on a whim, and it was the best whim of my life. Now the pentagram is powerless on me." I said.

"Cool. Just shows the power of God!" Abbot said.

I pulled on my shirt, and we went out to get kibbeltjes and mayo, some good purple kush, and a lot of weiss beer.

We were later stumbling by the water, and Abbot slurred, "Yyyyy-ooouuu are stupid. No one getttts a tat for just one guy. Thatttts stupid, and you're stuuupid too."

"Itttt was terrrrible for me. I lusted over disgusttttting, unnameable actttts, and pursued them at willll. I just hope what I remember is wrooong..." I said.

"Oh God, please let this poooor baby have a restful sleep..." Abbot said, as I began crying on her shoulder.

We got back home, she tucked me in, hushing my crying, saying shh, shh, and placed my princess wand in my hand. Abbot said, "It'll be ok. That spot is for your artist, or whoever you want, and not your dad. Heck, it's Chuck's home, and you've gotta treat it well."

"Thank you, Abbot. I really do think of being with women, sometimes. It's not a bad option, occasionally, if they make you feel nice." I said, snuggling in my bed.

"Aww. You make me sick, you little homo, coming on to me so sweetly. I don't sleep with my friends." Abbot said, kissed me on the cheek, and then stumbled to her bed, tripped onto it, and passed out immediately.

In the morning, Abbot was still passed out, and I had to work double time to clean up the rooms I missed the day before. Thankfully the Madame didn't notice, as she was busy on a business trip with potential partners, taking Francesca along. We were up to our own devices, but I knew the place sure as Hell had to be in better condition than when she left.

I got done around my usual time, and I went to a tattoo place to get something new.

I covered the upside down cross with a smiley face. Just a simple smiley face, black, that showed none of the upside down cross before.

I sighed in relief when it was over, not least because of the pain, and tipped the artist for being so professional. He nodded, and said there was a two for one deal, if I was interested.

Hmm... What should I get...

I got a heart, on my heart, with a keyhole in the center.

<h1 style="text-align:center">22</h1>

Francesca brought me to… to her sex pad.

It was filled with different styles of pork rinds, chicharrones, cracklins, fatbacks, and some of her own bizarre recipes. She said, offering me a sealed plastic bag, "So this is the new style of chip that I really like. What do you think?"

I just stared at the body on the bed. It was lifelike, albeit expressionless, it was nude, and completely stiff in the lower regions. I was surprised at such a… specimen, as the dummy had.

Francesca saw me looking, and said, "Oh, that's just Manny. Manny the Mannequin, get it? You gotta try him. He's got seven different settings!"

"…Seven?" I said.

"Well, you know sex is all about stages! Isn't he sweet? I can change his facial expression too, when we're in different moods!" Francesca said.

"…We're?" I said.

"…Manny and I? Don't you think he should get a mood, too? He thinks you're pleasant. Go on! Give him a feel!" Francesca said.

I nervously went and touched its skin. It felt like a real person, and I was a little afraid the mannequin was going to jump at my touch.

"Oh, don't be shy! Check out his member! I can switch it out for whatever I feel like currently! Big, small, even fantasy races like elves or hobgoblins!" Francesca said.

"...I didn't know elves had a different sort of penis..." I said, and slowly, touched its member. It felt like real life, almost pulsating-

And I jumped back, as it started vibrating.

Francesca laughed, and said, "Oh, he's very sensitive. He must really like you! I can make him do that myself if I press a button."

I didn't see any sort of button on the dummy, but I did see an anus on it.

I looked back at Francesca, who was chatting all about her new love of cooking, saying she just thought of if Manny could eat, what he would like to eat, and she was taking all sorts of cooking supplies out of cabinets, preparing pork rinds for me.

I sat at the table, with the dummy's strange presence, completely stiff, on the bed.

She was humming at the stove, turning on the heat, and I said, "...Francesca... This is kinda sad."

She looked at me, did a double take, and said, "The pork rinds? Yeah, I know! I'm stuck with all this stuff! But I'm sure I'll be able to unload it on some dummies, or even donate it and write it off as a tax break."

I said, "No... I mean the dummy."

"...Huh?" Francesca said, stopping cooking to look at me.

"It's just... I think you're great, you know that, right? You're smart, wise, powerful as hell, and obviously very creative. It's just... What on Earth drove you into the arms of a dummy over a real person?" I said.

She looked at the mannequin, then back at me nervously, and said, "I just got bored, is all! What's the harm in using some extra time? It's better than doing stuff with a prostitute, or even looking at porn, right? It doesn't harm anyone."

"...I think it's harming you." I said.

"Nonsense! Manny is as gentle as a fly! I mean he wouldn't harm a fly! Both! He's so caring, and sweet, and when we have dinner together- I mean, after I have dinner... alone... It's like sparks in the bed! No one else makes me feel like Manny does!" Francesca said, crossing her arms.

"I'm not sure what to say to you, Francesca, but I don't think you should give up on the human race, yet. There's all sorts of kind, sweet, and sensitive people out there-" I started saying.

But Francesca said, "You've gotta see this new model I'm working on! She's not done yet, but I'm making a mate for Manny, and us three will never be lonely again! I'll prove I'm not crazy!"

She went to the closet, and brought out a skeleton made of plastic, a female skeleton, with a human face with a wide open, gaping mouth.

I felt very disturbed, wondering why that was its facial expression that Francesca chose.

I intensely wanted to leave, as Francesca smiled at me, normally, kindly...

She stopped smiling as she saw the look on my face.

She looked down at the dummy, and stroked its cheek.

Then dropped the doll to the floor and began crying.

I hugged her, and we made a decision.

Francesca said, as we were carrying the dummy to the dumpster, "Can't... Can't I even use Manny one more time? He'll get lonely out there-"

"*No,* Francesca. It is not a *he.* It is a sex toy." I said.

"Ok... I'd chop off its part, just as a remembrance... but I could never do that to Manny..." Francesca said. We got to the dumpster, and Francesca said, "Wait. I want to say goodbye."

I shrugged. It was her crazy fantasy of a real person, and it's easier to let go if you say goodbye.

She said, "I'm sorry Manny, but I'm leaving you. You were the best husband I ever had, I mean that, and I'll always hold you close. But our time is over.

"I need to go out into the world again, and be with others. I'm sure I'll never meet another like you, but it is my time to leave.

"Of course I'll give you a kiss goodbye."

She kissed the dummy, long, passionately, in a heated embrace. It was a very intense moment.

Then she said, "Of course, just one more time is alright by me."

She then started stroking the dummy's man parts, and I had to gently take her hand away from its penis.

She sighed, we lifted the dummy up, and tossed it into the dumpster, right next to its mate.

We got back inside, and Francesca looked a little disoriented, and said, "Oh, I can't do this. They *need* me! I've got to go back out there-"

I said, "I think you should spend more time at the house, Francesca. Maybe the Madame can counsel you? I'm sure she'd know how to get this out of your system."

"But- But- Ok... I'll just take the pork rinds I like..." she said, grabbed a bag of chips, and we left the pad. She locked up, and pressed the key into my hand, and said, "I don't want to come back, and I don't want to be tempted. There are too many... memories... here."

I pocketed the key, and we went back to the house, walking through the streets back to the red light district. Francesca kept looking over her shoulder.

I patted her on the back, and said, "I think you did a very great thing today. And hey, if you keep it at a distance, don't get sucked up into the whole fantasy, you could actually make a very successful career in the sex toy market."

Francesca said, "...You think other people would like to have Mannys too?"

"Sure. Just for fun. It looked like quite a unique experience, and is probably better than any little toy made of plastic." I said.

"...Ok. I never thought of it like that. I just wanted to be with someone, one day, and the idea came to me after I saw this gorgeous man and his husband pass by the house, not even giving us a second thought. I followed them, and they were just seeing the sights, partners in love, partners in life. I basically stalked him for a while, using magic, until he left back on his flight, with his husband.

"I never... had such a fulfilling relationship as I did with my Manny. He understood, he cared, and always had time for me. He always thought I was beautiful, and showed it too." Francesca said.

"See, that sounds completely sane, and actually quite romantic, you lusting after a love you can't have. You could really write a romance story or two." I said.

"...I could? I mean, I don't know the first thing about writing. I'm just a human calculator." Francesca said.

"My artist tells me about writing, sometimes, and really when you write, it's like opening a piece of you you never thought you could embrace. It's magic, frankly, even if it is completely mundane. If you put your heart, your lust, and all the feelings of yours into a good story, it will be very relieving for you, and who knows? Maybe other people will enjoy it too." I said.

"I'd like that. Thank you, for your help, Mary. I usually only sleep at the house if I have a lot of work to do in the morning and had a late night, but I wouldn't mind being with the girls again." Francesca said.

We got back to the house, and Francesca quickly squeezed me into a hug, and I hugged her back.

23

I ate with Tas, Francesca, Abbot, Malena... and Diane. Diane ate silently as the rest of us talked, chatting about what we were going to do today.

Abbot said, "I'm gonna have a party today! Well, a work party, but still! Poppin' out of a cake and everything. I think they're into bukkake, so I'm going to have a loooong day. I'm glad they paid in advance."

Tas said, "That sounds great, Abbot. Are they all supplied?"

Abbot said, "Nah, but I'll send them to a 'friend of a friend,' you, beforehand. I could use a couple bumps myself, just to get in the party mood."

Tas said, "Great. I love our rich, upper class society. There's nothing like friendly faces from home to unload the good stuff on. They pay premium, even though they think they're getting the best deal. How's the laundry business going, Francesca?"

Francesca said, "Oh, the pork rinds are so good, I can put any amount down from your deals and we get clean as a whistle. They're actually quite popular in Asia, surprisingly."

Malena said, "You three are really the powerhouses here. I've just got a few lovers wrapped around me, the usuals..."

Abbot shook her head, and said, "If we had a popularity contest in our work, I think you'd win, Malena. You've got those guys out for you *hard.* They open up their worst fantasies to you, and to you alone. When you tell me about some of your jobs, I get a little jealous because they're so intimate. What did that one guy say when you told him-"

Malena giggled, and said, "Shush, you! It's our secret. Just because he likes to be a dragon, and me his sacrificial virgin- Oops. I've said too much."

We laughed, and I said, "And I'm the maid."

Abbot poked me, sitting beside her, and said, "We all love a nice, clean home to come back to, Mary."

Diane ate silently, looking at her food. I tried to open up a conversation with her. I said, "So, Diane… How's the new act?"

She looked at me, and looked back at her food.

She said to me, "I found a crumb in the bed. Clean better."

"…Ok. I change the sheets after every act-" I said.

"I think that's fine. I'm going to take another shower." Diane said, and cleaned up her plate, and left.

We looked at her walk away, and Tas said, "…She's been taking a lot of showers, even before work…"

Malena said, "Well, yeah! It's her birthday today! It's the worst day of her life!"

I said, "I thought those were good days?"

Malena shook her head, and said, "Not for Diane. She doesn't look at life as a good thing for her. The only reason she doesn't pop herself off is because of the Madame."

Tas said, "I've been trying to show her a good day, all and all, gave her some of the stuff she likes… but I don't know… I feel like antidepressants won't really cheer her up. It's not like it'll get her high or anything."

Francesca said, "Maybe she just needs a day off?"

Abbot said, "No… I think if she doesn't do anything it'll be an even worse day. I wish there weren't people like… You know. Who did that to Diane when she was a kid."

I said, "Child molesters?"

Abbot said, "Yeah. Those kind. Before Diane came here, they didn't understand her at all, not her powers, not her mind, and were going to lock her up in a loony bin for the rest of her life in a Russian cell. Until the Madame found her. She got the best lawyers to get her out of that shithole, finding her sane enough even though they wanted to 'cure' her."

I said, "Are the hospitals bad places in Russia? Luke, my artist, mentioned the ones in the U.S. a couple times. He would've been locked up in one of them for a loooong time, if he didn't get the legal aid he needed. Would've been labeled criminally insane, and then shoved aside for good."

Abbot said, "I don't know about Russia… from what Diane has told me… But they're actually quite good in Holland, focusing on rehabilitation primarily. I don't know what the ones in America are like, but in Russia they were also going to treat Diane indefinitely. Something about hearing someone say they've got magic powers puts a little bit of an 'insane' label on you…"

"How did the Madame get her out of that?" I asked.

Abbot said, "Well, Diane's powers, the ones she's good at, aren't about throwing fire in your face or making sparkly rainbows. It's not visible, but when you do something, you never know if it's really Diane making you do it. The Madame knew, however, and showed her how to act the part as a 'sane' person. Magic was the one thing that Diane had, in the loony bin."

"Maybe I'll go see if I can cheer her up. I got some weed I like, and maybe she'd like a toke with me." I said, getting up, as the rest started talking about something else.

I found Diane in our shared sleeping room getting dressed. I gasped as I saw the scars on her back for just a second, but when I blinked, they were gone.

I said, "So, Diane! Happy Birthday. Want to have some birthday weed?"

She put on her skimpy clothes, clothes for the late night morning show that she would take off in the act, and looked back at me.

"You think that will make me happy?" she said.

"I think it's very relaxing." I said.

"...You're just giving it to me? You're not selling it? I didn't suggest you give me your possessions." Diane said.

"I just want to be nice, is all!" I said.

"I don't think weed will help." Diane said.

"Please, allow me to do something for you. Anything. I want this to be a happy day for you." I said.

"You can take off your clothes and fuck yourself, if you want. That'd make me happy." Diane said.

"Ok! I'll do just that!" I said, and took off my clothes, and began fucking myself with my wand-

Wait. The fuck am I doing?

Diane watched, as I continued.

"A little more insertion with the wand. This is exactly what I'm going to do in the show." Diane said.

I smiled, as I put the wand in.

I was happy, looking into Diane's eyes. She made me feel like I had the best birthday in the world-

Um. Mary Jane. This is Chuck.

Oh! Hello! Should I put it in deeper-

Remember that one couple who tried to help you? Not everyone wants your help. You are the Princess, and do not have to take anyone's abuse.

I looked down at the wand, sopping in my hand-

I took it out, and turned it into a sword, facing Diane.

"Don't do that to me again, Diane." I said, wielding the sword at her.

"Don't ask me to be happy. Now you know how that feels." Diane said, and walked away.

I shivered on the bed, cleaned myself, and put back on my clothes.

Late in the evening, I caught Diane's end show. She did exactly what I had done to myself. I was fully prepared against any of her disorientation, clutching my princess wand close.

There were only five people here, including myself. Usually she attracted viewers like flies, but I think that might've been a fad, something about 'new artforms.'

So she compensated for that, and made each viewer feel like they were really with her, looking into their eyes, winking, fondling a tit on a request.

She even looked into my eyes, but only glared at me.

At the end, the bidding began.

Yes, this is a thing, and at the end show of Diane's, each person bid to sleep with her.

I raised my hand as well, as Abbot took offers from the bidders of Diane.

Abbot said, "...Erhem... The Dutiful Duchess Diane isn't taking female offers tonight..."

I stood up, and said, "I don't care. I'll double the bid, then."

Abbot said, "...It's your choice with your money, I guess. What do you say, Duchess?"

Diane looked at Abbot, back at me, and nodded. The other spenders left the building with regret and unsated desires.

I went into a back room with Diane, and she began undressing for me.

I said, "No. I don't want any of that. Since I paid for you, we're just going to talk, ok? I really don't want to end up hurting myself if I piss you off accidentally."

She looked back at me, put back on the top, and sat on the bed with me.

"I could make you fuck me, if that's what I wanted." Diane said.

I started a cigarette, lighting it with my flame, and sat smoking beside a barely clothed Diane.

"I know. That's what makes it terrifying being alone with you. I know that most people can't tell if they're aroused, or you're just making them aroused. There's a difference, maybe slightly… but it's with what you can do." I said.

"Yes, there is a difference. I'm not just going to open up to you since you paid a normal price." Diane said.

"It's really normal? I had to empty out a month's worth of work on you… Man, I thought that was expensive, for only an hour." I said.

"I used to get more. I'm not having trouble with disorientation… I just took a dive in popularity. People say I'm cold. They say I'm heartless. They're missing the best night of their life by passing up on me.

"I know how to please someone, of both genders, because they used me to please themselves.

"Let's get this over with… You want to know how I was raped, don't you. Is that your fetish?" Diane said.

"I don't. I don't want to tell people how I was raped, either, so you can keep your secrets. My father is the Devil, Diane. I wonder if you can understand how that feels." I said.

"...Maybe. I- I didn't think of that... I'm not sure if what you felt is worse or better than me, as I was traded with multiple people, like a toy." Diane said.

"I got a new tat. Wanna see? It's a happy smiley." I said, pulled down my pants, and showed off my tat.

"Why are you showing me your vagina?" Diane said.

"Because it used to not even belong to me. It always did, but I didn't believe it before. This tattoo shows that it is mine. I know, that's sad... but-" I said.

Diane frowned sadly, and said, "No, I can understand."

"I want you to know that you can feel comfortable around me, and that I won't push on your barriers. I think we've got to stick together, all of us, since we all belong to ourselves, and not who we rent out our services to." I said.

"Like the Madame. She is my mother, in a sense. She is my saviour. I owe her everything, even though she set me free." Diane said.

"And you still want to be groped and fondled with your freedom?" I said.

"Not always. I was thinking about opening a flower shop if I could've saved up enough to live comfortably. This is just work." Diane said.

"You can always end the work, change jobs, even if it's difficult-" I said.

"I could've always ended it, too. I can give up this life, my life, and be done working." Diane said.

"I think you can live for a while longer, and find peace." I said.

"I want to be cremated. I wonder why you thought to see my show?" Diane said.

"...Because I wanted to catch you in this alone time?" I said.

"You're going to kill me tonight, because you want to. I assure you, it *will* be suicide, so do not feel guilty." Diane said.

"What? No, I would never do that." I said.

"This is a last testament to you, Mary Jane. You are my suicide note.

"I hate them all. Every single person who has intruded upon me. All of them. If I could I would blatantly sew my orifices up, so none could broach upon me.

"I love you the most, Madame, because you have never intruded upon me.

"I don't want to live anymore. The memories are too painful, and the people in it are always there. I cannot shut them out, and they are still intruding upon me.

"Goodbye. This is the kiss of death, Mary Jane, and I accept it." Diane said.

Then she kissed me, as I raised my hands in fire.

I was going to hug her, and accept her embrace, as I was in my own flame.

I knew I wanted to hug her, to tell her it is ok.

But all I could feel was my flame.

I denied her death, and put my hands by my side.

She looked at me frightened, and said, "You would really let me suffer??"

I said, "Yes. *For this life is suffering.*

"Life was always worse than Hell. And I deny you mercy, because I am the Devil's Daughter.

"Look into my eyes. They contain all of Hell.

"You have not kissed true death... you have kissed eternal damnation.

"And I damn you to live."

She burst out crying, and I let my demon parts fade again.

I walked out of the room, as she continued to cry.

24

I told what Diane said to the Madame, and the Madame looked taken aback. "I don't know what she's thinking sometimes, it is our arrangement, and this is heartrending. Where is she now?"

"Abbot is taking care of her with Malena. She needs a bit of a break, maybe some flowers." I said.

"I must see her. Take tomorrow off, Mary." the Madame said, and rushed out the door.

I went to bed, as I heard faint crying coming from the nurse's, Diane's crying.

I talked to Francesca a bit, to tell her what happened.

"She never cries." Francesca said, "Absolutely never."

I said, "Maybe that's what's good for her..."

"But seriously. You *damned her to live??* Sounds kind of... Actually it sounds appropriate. I'm proud of you, Mary." Francesca said, "Now, goodnight, I'm missing my doll, and really just need to sleep off the urges. I've got work tomorrow... Stupid pig rinds..." and she snuggled up in her bed.

I went to sleep, and heard my sweet song in my dreams, I smiled, skipping down the path, and met Luke feeding my dream chickens.

"These guys are kind of nice, when they're sweet. Nothing like real chickens." Luke said, as I sat beside him.

I snuggled against him, as the music played, and he wrapped an arm around me.

We just sat there for a while, as he fed my big eyed, pretty eyelashed dream chickens.

I ate some of the grain he was throwing out, just reached a hand in the bag. Mmm… That hits the spot.

"So how are the voices?" I asked, "I just heard one in the bushes over there. Is that yours or mine?"

Luke shrugged, and said, "Probably mine. Sounds like John, to me."

John came out of the bushes, and well, he was shrouded in shadow. That's a good thing, when the voices take less of a physical appearance, and you can't even remember what they look like in a dream.

"Hi John. Did you come to be fed, too?" Luke said.

John didn't say a thing, and walked off.

"They've become kind of quieter, lately. I really hope that they're just gone for good, but I'd be deceiving myself looking for an end to my torment." Luke said.

"That's life. It's continuous, everlasting torment." I said.

We sighed in comfort.

"Is this song on a loop?" Luke asked.

"I thought you put it on?" I said.

We listened to the sweet song play eternally.

We decided to take a walk further into the forest.

We pushed past the dream brush, and I said, "I suppose even nice things can be torment if you have them all the time. I wonder how they fix that, up in Heaven? Maybe every nice thing is new."

A branch hit Luke in the face, and he said, "I think they do stuff with a challenge. Like give their angels jobs or something."

"Might be nice." I said, "Better than being aimless in Hell."

"I know you've told me a lot about your past... But do you still need to talk about it? We can, anytime you like." Luke said, as we got to a pool in the forest, and sat beside it.

I sighed, and said, "I know I told you I wasn't raped... but I was. It just wasn't like what you expect, being chased down and forced on. It was twisty, and disturbing. It's like someone is fucking with your mind as well as your body, and the only way out is to give in, but it still doesn't end even if you do."

Luke clenched his fist, as I continued.

"It's twisty, and you're *supposed* to trust that person, but you can't, and you don't, but you try. In the end... well, in the end you're in an even worse Hell. It doesn't feel good, even if your body is being stimulated.

"You know that knot in your stomach you get from certain feelings? You always have that knot, when you're stuck in this sort of relationship."

"...I can feel that. Thank you for telling me." Luke said.

"Thank you for listening... Can you hold me? I'm starting to shake." I said.

Luke held me by the pool, and I could see that he was crying gently.

"Are you ok?" I asked.

"I'm just so angry. And there's nothing I can do about it." Luke said.

"You can be here for me, now. That's all I ask." I said.

Luke sighed, wiped off the slight tears, and we continued to sit by the pool, watching the dreams inside of it that other people were having.

Abbot was talking to her long lost puppy, cuddling him in delight.

Francesca was meeting someone new, and talking in delight.

Malena wasn't dreaming of anything, in blissful delight.

Tas was a woman, feeling her parts, sighing in delight.

Diane was crying, even in a dream... but in delight.

Luke held me, and I held him. He told me a joke, and we laughed together in delight.

25

Malena and I were hanging out on my day off, just going to an art museum actually. We looked at a lot of old, classic art, with a lot of nudity in them.

Malena said, "Oh! This one, let me try this one."

She waved her knife, and turned into an old classical style art figure, smiling one of those old smiles.

I laughed, and said, "Oh, I'm gonna be this guy. I can't do the actual body stuff like you can, but I can do a good illusion."

I poofed myself with the wand, in the appearance of a big, nude, bearded man.

Malena held my hand, and we walked around the art gallery, as an old classical couple, laughing to each other as people stared at our artstyle and my nude figure.

A security guard came over to us, gasped, and said, "De kunst komt tot leven. Is dit het einde van de wereld?" and ran away from us.

We laughed, and disappeared out the doors.

We sat by a canal, and I said, "I used to be able to walk around nude, without anyone caring. I think it was the magic of Hell or something that was keeping me protected."

Malena said, "You ascended to Heaven, after you fell from Hell. Perhaps that is the Earth."

"That sounded cool." I said.

"I take poetry lessons. It's just a way to use an extra bit of cash without gorging myself on snacks." Malena said.

"Can you recite some more?" I asked.

Malena said, "Well, I do know Milton, I know some Spanish poets too you might be fond of, from my homeland, but I'll just make up something new for you.

"Avast! Ye scurvy dogs, fighting amongst ye self, like scurviest hogs...

"The whore care not, which one is bigger, she careth only for the biggest spender...

"So yeh limp pricks and sick dicks, bring all ye can, the whore is hungry, like an open clam...

"The wealthiest is the poorest, for he has naught to spend, and the whore loves him, though does not show it...

"As she takes every dick, seaman on land, she sucks and fucks, but thinks only of one man...

"The wealthiest poorman, who has naught to spend, which she meets in the alley, and jerks with one hand...

"There be more sailors to fuck, more cash to grab, yet she loves only this one man.

"Thus is life, for the whore on land."

"I like that the guy she loves only gets a handjob. Seems nice." I said.

"Well, of course all the old poets would say he would just get a kiss, but I upped it up a notch. I mean, poor guy's probably envisioning her all through the voyage, as she is envisioning him! Sounds cruel to leave it on a kiss." Malena said.

"So why doesn't she sleep with him then?" I said.

"Well she's gotta keep a reputation! She can't be the *free* whore! Men wouldn't take her seriously! Just giving a handjob is risky enough." Malena said.

"...Is this sailor a real person?" I asked.

Malena blushed, and said, "Well... I embellished a bit. He's not a sailor, a soldier, or anyone that goes on long voyages. He just lives in the east, and is really struggling right now. His wife doesn't even-"

"His wife?" I said.

Malena blushed harder, and said, "They stopped doing it! Like, years ago! And really, I believe him. Just how he acts around me, so nervous all the time..."

"You can't seek him out with clarity to find if he's telling the truth?" I asked.

"I'm not really... that good at all the ethereal magic. I usually just test if people are true by their body language, like Tas does." Malena said.

"Want me to check?" I said.

"...You could? That would really give me a reason to either end the relationship or step it up a notch." Malena said.

"Ok, so you said he lives in the east... What's he look like?" I asked.

"He's got a glass eye, and has luscious golden hair, which he recently got a haircut of. His nose looks like an eagle's beak, and his lips... Very plush." Malena said.

"Ok, I'll look for glass eye, golden hair, eagle nose, plush lips. That *is* very descriptive... but I'll need to know something about his interests, something to draw me to his soul." I said.

"He likes me? I don't know. I guess he said he liked cars. Wanted something like a Ford 69. I thought he was just suggesting 69ing, but maybe that's a thing." Malena said.

"Got a name?" I asked.

"Bram." Malena said.

So I closed my eyes, and looked for Malena's poor man.

I hooked onto the desire for a Ford 69, and found him.

I saw him looking at himself in the mirror, worried about his haircut and his glass eye. He got the glass eye because he was an idiot on the job one time, and welded without a helmet. A spark got in his eye and damaged it, and they had to remove the eye.

He kissed his wife when he got out of the bathroom. It was a very cold kiss.

He said some stuff in Dutch to her, and she said some stuff back. Pretty soon they were yelling at each other, and then the baby woke up.

The wife scolded Bram, and went to the baby.

Bram sighed, and sat on the couch with his face in his hands, amidst the piles of bills scattered on the couch.

I guess he was a poor man in a tough spot. But I wanted to see if he and his wife were still intimate. That was the root of Malena's and his relationship.

I sat in his apartment, invisible to him, and smoked a cigarette.

They had a nice dinner, his wife and him, and they said their apologies to each other.

Could this just be an off day for them?

They went to bed, and did not kiss, or touch, or anything. They simply lay with their backs to each other, with the baby in a crib beside them.

I wondered how old the baby was.

I confronted him in his dream, after he fell asleep thinking of Malena.

"So. Are you really a poor man who loves a whore?" I said from behind him, in his dream where he was trapped in his house, with no doors or windows.

He jumped, looked back at me, and said, "Are you an American debt collector?"

"No. I'm the maid. I've come to either sponge this relationship up, or let it grow. Your words can make the difference, and I'll know if you're lying, so save us both time and tell the truth. Do you love Malena?" I said.

He didn't say anything.

I sighed, and said, "Look, I can also go deeper into your head-"

"I cannot say one way or the other. If I say that I love her, then my wife will leave me. If I say I do not, I will be trapped in this house with no other way out. There is one nice thing in my life, and it is that brothel worker."

"Why? You just like getting your jimmies juiced?" I said.

"...Jimmies juiced? Is this American slang?" he said.

"Sorry, forgot how we have different euphemisms. You like getting off with Malena. That sound right?" I said.

"Get... off? I am sorry, my English is not very good." he said.

I sighed, and said, "Handjob. She jerks you off for free. You like that?"

"Oh! Yes. Are you going to do that to me too? It has been so long for me without a woman-" he said, and unbuckled his belt.

"No, goddamnit... What are you doing?" I said.

"She always kisses me before we start. It is our tradition." he said, trying to kiss me.

"Goddamnit, I've seen enough." I said, and opened my eyes.

Malena was sleeping on the bench beside me, and I woke her up in the night.

She shot open her eyes, and said, "What'd he say?? What did my poor sailor say??"

"He wanted me to do what you do in a dream, Malena. Dude's scum." I said, starting another cigarette.

"...Well, it *was* a dream. You mean you don't get off in dreams with strangers, too?" she said.

"Listen, trust me, he'd take anyone who does what you do. He doesn't love *you,* he loves the action you give him." I said, as we got up and went back to the house.

"Oh... That makes me kind of sad." Malena said.

"Next time you charge him for a normal handy, and then put him out of your mind like all the rest." I said.

"I guess… But did I tell you about my dragon guy?? He's the best, and I think with this next outfit I got, we should have so much fun!!" Malena said, and then chatted about her roleplaying she did with a customer.

I shrugged. I guess Malena just was a loving individual.

26

Diane was taking a break from prostitution, and opened up a tulip stand down the road, with the Madame's full support. She still stayed at the house, but actually smiled when she got home.

I asked her, "So how are you doing with the flowers? Not still mad at me, are you?"

"They are very peaceful creatures, and I like letting people look at them, even though most don't buy very often. I want to tell you that I think of you as a saviour as well, Devil's Daughter. If my soul will go somewhere when I die, I hope it goes into your hands." Diane said.

I smiled.

That's how you steal a soul. You don't make stupid, crazy deals like my dad does. You just show kindness.

I talked to my boyfriend at our phone time, and he said he had a little slump in art, in between the pics of me, but sent me a picture he drew... of Abbot.

"Well, she suggested that she'd like to pose for me a while back, and I thought-" Luke said over the phone.

"Oh. Dream pose? Why... *Abbot??*" I said.

"She's very professional with her body, so don't worry about anything! Didn't come onto me once! She just-" Luke said.

"Got nude before you and stuck her butt out, right? That's what it looks like she's doing in this picture..." I said.

"Er, I m-mean, she s-said I c-could do some of the other girls too! Something to help your home, since they're helping you! A little calendar, or s-something!" Luke said.

"...Alright. It better be classy. I don't want to see pics of you going down on her or anything. That's *our* thing." I said.

"...Right. All class. Although if they're up to it maybe they can-" Luke said.

"I mean it, Luke. All class." I said.

"...Ok. Love you, Jane!" Luke said.

I sighed, and said, "Love you too, Luke, you big dummy. I can't wait 'til you come here soon!"

"Me too! It'll be fun coming back to Holland. Oh, one thing... about your one friend... The one who's really a guy-" Luke said.

"...What about her?" I asked.

"How does she want me to draw her? Abbot suggested I show the truth, but I'm wondering what the truth actually is." Luke said.

"Look inside yourself, and you'll see. Later, Luke. Don't fall in love with the drawings, ya hear!" I said.

He laughed, and said, "That only happened once. When I drew you. Later, Jane."

I smiled, and hung up.

Everyone somehow knew now that Tas had a penis. I hadn't told a soul. It definitely wasn't obvious, but rumors go around, and some inspect those rumors, and then you have some like Abbot who blatantly tell everyone after they do.

I caught her saying in the break room, our dining room, "I mean, it's fine if he's a bi guy, what's the big deal? He's the best coworker I've had, so professional... but it does make me wonder what else he's hiding."

I said to her, "Shut it, you. You don't know how difficult it is to be torn in twain."

"Well, I mean, he could *really* work with us, if he wanted to! People get a kick out of transgenders all the time! It's a niche fetish, but a very popular one." Abbot said, sipping at her tea with the others.

"I don't think that's what Tas would want." I said.

"Who cares! He could rake it in! I've gotta tell him about this one deal with this couple I know, he could be their dom/sub, at the same time! I'll go ask-" Abbot said.

"No, Abbot. Don't make me hurt you. Let Tas find out what she wants herself." I said.

Abbot snickered at me, and said, "What? Now that your boytoy found a new muse, you find a new boytoy? You are la femme fatale…"

"Quiet, Abbot. You were always the degenerate, and even your God knows… Why else do you think he blessed you with your 'talents?' You are filth, not even worthy to be stepped on." I said.

Abbot growled at me, and snarled, "Go back to Hell, you ugly bitch, because no one is going to be fucking you on Earth anymore. Not even boytoy. Why else do you think he sent you away? I gave him that handjob, Mary Jane. And he still loves me more than you."

"You ugly SLUT!!" I yelled, and flew at her, tackling her to the ground, beating the shit out of her-

"Oops. You attacked a phantasm. Best get that bleeding fist checked out… HAHAHA!!" Abbot said, from across the room, and walked away.

I got up from where I saw Abbot, as her illusion disappeared, and grumbled, letting my demon parts fade again. My fist was bleeding from smashing it so hard against the ground.

I let the nurse, Diamond, heal it, and told her of my frustrations with Abbot.

"She was lying, you know." Diamond said, as she touched the bleeding fist with the scalpel, letting it heal gently.

"How can you tell? This makes me so frustrated, and I don't know what to do-" I said.

"Did your artist ever tell you a name for that brothel worker from his past?" Diamond asked.

"...No, but he said he couldn't remember her name." I said.

"And I doubt if it happened that Abbot would remember his. It obviously wasn't a very satisfactory experience, if he couldn't even remember the woman's name, so why should you worry?" Diamond said.

"...I guess that's true. But why is Abbot such a bitch behind everyone's back! I just want it to come back and bite her." I said.

"We oftentimes find flaws in those we care for, it's how we care, as we want them to be the best version of themselves that they can. I think if you tell Abbot this, she *may* listen to what you have to say. It's probably healthier talking things out, rather than trying to beat her up." Diamond said.

"Ok... I'll talk to her later then. I've got to go do my job, thank you, Diamond." I said.

"Don't mention it. But... One thing. May I *please* feel your wings? I was wondering what material they are made of." Diamond said.

"...Ok. I guess." I said, and put out my wings, and let Diamond stroke them.

"My... Like no other leather I've ever felt. It must be some sort of hellbeast, perhaps alike to one of the higher archdemons..." she said, as she continued to stroke the wings.

"...You know about different classes of demons?" I asked.

"Oh yes. They've been some of my best teachers, and sometimes most charming companions. Thank you for this sample of memory, Mary Jane. It will serve me well." Diamond said.

I shrugged, as she began writing something down on paper, and left the infirmary.

Diamond called out to me, "Oh! And if you see Tas, let her know that I can perform the procedure on her whenever she's ready!"

Her procedure?

I gasped, and ran out to find Tas outside the house, as she was talking with Abbot.

Abbot said, "Why not? But you and I could really-"

"I'm sorry, Abbot. But I want to try something new. *Really* new. I think it would be nice to be normal me... I've been in the middle for a long, long time, and-" Tas said.

I yelled out to Tas, "Your procedure is ready! Go get em, champ! I can't wait to see you when you're fully-"

"Er, Mary... This is not a good time-" Tas said.

Abbot hugged Tas, and said, "I don't *care* what gender you are... We can-"

I said, "Quit being la stupid bitch, Abbot. You don't have to try and make me jealous again."

Tas stopped hugging Abbot, and said, "I'm sorry, Abbot but I... I just... and then you go and tell my secret to everyone you can..."

Abbot said, "It's a big secret! And I love your secret! Don't throw it away on a fancy! God loves you just as you are, as I do! I didn't mean to let my tongue slip, I just was proud of it, as I am of you!"

"...I'm going through with this, Abbot. See you on the other side." Tas said, and walked away to the nurse's, as Abbot burst out crying.

"So you were really just jealous of me?" I said.

Abbot said, "What do you care... I liked that guy ever since I met him... and now he's going to be some *freak*.

"He told me about you and him. You don't pass up on a soldier like Tas. You get down on your knees in love, and thank God to be so lucky. He gets me off just with that silver, no, golden tongue of his…"

"I thought I was going gay, when I met him. Then, I catch him in the bathroom, pulling out his beautiful secret… and I knew it was God's will.

"Why should you care, Devil's Daughter?"

"I believe it is Tas's choice, and that you are interfering with her freedom." I said.

"He *can be free with me!!* I had so many fantasies, so much plans…" Abbot said, and slumped against the house wall, wiping off her tears.

She was soon sitting on the ground, and I sat beside her and started a cigarette. I said, "Well, maybe she'll still like you as a woman?"

"I only do that stuff with women for work… It's not really as enjoyable to me, and most of the time they can tell that, and go to one of the others. I haven't had a *single* true love in all my life… I guess I've got a good score at that, why break it, eh?" Abbot said, starting a cig.

I shrugged, and we just sat smoking for a while. What I wanted to say to Abbot seemed unimportant now, because she was obviously in love, the way she whimpered every few seconds while smoking.

Eventually Tas asked us if we could see her.

She undressed before us, showing off all her tattoos, and new female parts.

"I still can't get pregnant… but I think this is a good compromise. It feels so… good." Tas said, posing before us.

Abbot sniffled, and said, "You're a beautiful woman, Tas."

27

My artist, Luke, had finally arrived! I had invited him to come visit, ever since I got the idea of using Francesca's sex pad as a place for him to stay, and Luke upped our idea of romantic outings, sadly, by deciding to get some work done while he was here.

He was going to sketch the girls in his now studio, Francesca first because she wanted to show him around, and the two really bonded when talking about art.

"You have a sort of wild streak in your art. Frankly it seems a little messy to me, but I can really tell you put a lot of care into the stroke of the lines." Francesca said, looking at the drawing of her.

"Thanks. I like your star tat! It's those little details that really make the figure interesting. All of your talismans are so cool, and I like you posing with the pencil, Francesca." Luke said.

Francesca smacked her own butt, and said, "I got this tat in my college years. I never wanted anything too fancy. It's not dumb, is it?"

"No, not at all! Shows class, actually." Luke said.

"Eh hem." I said, "If you two are done, can we please go and get some food?"

Francesca said, "Of course, of course. Sorry about being a third wheel, but maybe I'll have better luck meeting someone with you guys." and put back on her clothes.

The two were very professional towards each other, but still I knew that Luke *liked* drawing naked women because he *liked* naked women. I didn't worry too much about it that he was seeing my friends naked, but sometimes I wondered if he saw something he liked better in them than me.

As we talked, he dispelled my fears with that comfortable humor, smiling crooked teeth, and talked to me like I was his best friend. I think we were best friends, actually. It made me feel good that I could be with someone who mattered this way to me, and not only end up sleeping with people I hate like Abbot did.

We met Abbot and Tas at the restaurant. Abbot shoved down her feelings of disgust for her own gender, and decided to try and love a new member of the female counterpart. You could tell she was nervous as Tas touched her comfortably in some spots as we ate, a touch of the hands, a squeeze around the waist... and then the kiss.

We saw it when it happened, them sitting by the fountain outside the restaurant, and Abbot had her eyes opened in surprise, looking like she didn't know what to do, but slowly, gently, kissed Tas back.

Eventually they just made out at the fountain, and we watched for a while. Abbot stopped kissing as she noticed us, straightened up, and got up with Tas. "What are you all staring at? Haven't you ever seen a woman kiss a transgender woman? Let's get drunk."

We went to a bar, meeting Malena with her dragon guy friend. They were seeing each other outside of business! Malena said, "I gave Bram a real eye, for all his dedicated love, and then broke off the relationship. He claimed he would marry me for what I did for him, but I told him to stick with his wife, and he sighed, walking away. He was a good sailor... but I think he'll be able to get past that unfortunate incident with his eye, and start up his life again."

Francesca was successfully flirting with someone, and then someone else walked out of the bathroom.

Francesca's dummy, with different colored eyes, one a glass eye, with an undead rooster on his shoulder. He went up to us, as I was the first person to notice them, and the dummy said, "How do you like me now, bitches. I got a real one!!"

The dummy then pulled down his pants, and flashed us.

The dummy then howled to the ceiling, like some damn dog.

Abbot stuttered, "M-Maarty?"

Francesca stuttered, "M-Manny?"

Malena gasped, and said, "That's Bram's glass eye."

"And my penis!!" Tas shouted.

"With my rooster on your shoulder. What is it you want, demon? Leave us be." I said.

The dummy said, "I'm no demon. I'm worse. I'm all of you. All your *failures!!* If I didn't have such a cute little puppy dog soul, I'd tell my rooster friend to sic you all. All of you can fuck off, and fuck yourself too. But not until I get into the real root of how much I hate all of you.

"Ya wanna know what happened to me, Abbot? Ya wanna know what happened to your dog? You locked me in a box, trying to be a stupid magician. When you opened the box the next day, I was gone! Wowhow! You must be a *sorceress!!* Your fucking mother just let you believe this, and threw me out in the trash before you knew. You fucking killed me!!

"And you, you fucking stupid, ugly, bookworm. Francesca, you think we had *any* connection? I was a fucking dummy. Literally. I couldn't move, I couldn't even think!! You were playing with toys, Francesca. Stupid, fucking, toys, and you believed they were real, just like when you were a child and believed your pictures could move. You're just old enough to fuck them now, and just shameless enough to have no regret of it. My nose would grow ten times longer if I said I loved you.

"But I got something else that grows when I say that. Heya, Tas. You gave up on a real, fucking normal body. You tweaked it out with all sorts of hormones, even stuffed your penis away, so no one would ever see it. You have no pride in your body. No pride *on* your body, now. I'm gonna do what you never did with this dick… I'm gonna fuck the entire world.

"And woohoo! Malena! The side action! I knew when I saw you, I saw an easy lay. I cheated on my wife constantly, and that's why she doesn't do it with me anymore! I thought I'd get you in the bed with one fucking hand! But all I got was hand! You were always a free whore, and nothing more. An easy handy, and then I can go back home, close my eyes, and be able to sleep at night.

"And the worst bitch of the lot, who thinks she's too good to even be a working girl. The one who thinks she's too good for the *Earth!* The maid! The steals your soul, tries to kill you, Devil's Maid! My friend on my shoulder told me all about *you.* You see, when you steal a soul… they take a bit of you as well. You wonder why your dad's all fucked up? You're looking at it, on my shoulder, babe. The end goal of stealing souls isn't to play God… It's to kill the unkillable. You stole my friend's death!

"I hate you all! Remember me, for I will always be around… I am your failure, and your failure is eternal. Now fuck yourself, and fuck off too."

The undead rooster cockadoodle dooed in that horrible manner, and our horrible failure left the bar.

Francesca

28

The dragon guy said he had to go, but hugged Malena goodbye. Malena said, "S-See you sometime?"

"I don't know... Maybe. That was really weird, what that one guy said. I... Maybe I should try and not be a dragon anymore, and try to move on..." he said, and shambled away.

We walked down the street in silence.

Luke said, "...Maybe you need to put your failure to rest."

I said, "I think we should kill it."

Abbot stuttered, "B-But he's Maarty. Maarty's soul. I can't k-kill my dog again..."

Francesca said, "...That was always what I'd dream of Manny doing, actually getting up and talking to me... I never knew he wanted to say such harsh things..."

Tas held Abbot's hand, and said, "Y-You think I'm beautiful, right? This wasn't a mistake, was it?"

Abbot kissed her on the cheek, and said, "I think you're the most beautiful woman alive, and I didn't even like women. You changed my mind, even before I knew you once had a penis."

Tas said, "Th-Thank you. I feel like all my words have fallen away from me. I can't even use magic, guys. I just put up an act, my whole time. I say shit like words are powerful, language is art, but... maybe it doesn't mean anything..."

Luke said, "I think there's a lot of power in words, and the mundane can be just as strong as magic, in most any scenario."

"Yeah." I said, "That's what a normal guy says. I lived in Hell. I brought a chicken to life... I'm more powerful than all of you combined-"

Francesca said, "And you fucked yourself with it, just like us, just like Manny said."

I said, "...I guess that's true. I- I'm sorry."

Francesca said, "Don't mention it. Ever. I'm going back to the house now... I have work in the morning... real work, and not cleaning up other people's messes."

Francesca huffed, and left us.

Malena said, "S-So Bram was really using me the whole time? But... he was so sweet."

Tas said, "Men think with their dick, Malena. It's... stupid. You were kind of stupid for giving stuff away for free. I've hooked you up with people *so* many times, good choices, lots of cash, but you fucking fell in love with some bum who wouldn't even pay you."

Malena said, "...I'm not only a whore. I have real, human needs, for real, human connections."

"Screw it. Then quit. I'm going home, too. See you later, Abbot." Tas said, kissed Abbot, and left to her own home.

Abbot sighed out, after Tas was out of view, and said, "That was the most difficult date of my life."

I said, "Oh, get the fuck over it, Abbot. Just because you're in love with God doesn't mean you can't love someone just because they have the same genitalia as you."

"I do love God. And I feel in twain as well, knowing that I have committed to a sinful relationship for real. It twists my head around, and I'm sure it'll pop off if I'm not careful. I miss my dog… and I wish he was still a dog again… and I'm so sad… I'm just going to walk around for a while, by myself…" Abbot said, and shuffled away.

Malena said, "S-So what do you guys want to do? Let's keep this party going! Yeah!"

Luke and I looked at each other, and I shrugged. Luke said to Malena, "Want to… Want me to draw you, I guess? I guess we can do that for a while."

Malena said, "Great! I've never had this happen before, where people all just ditched each other because they're mad and sad. Usually I can fix that, make people happy just with my presence… Were people just being too nice to me?"

I said, "I don't think all the time. You really do make most people feel very good about themselves, because they feel good about you."

"Thank you. I don't think you're just a maid, either. Just being at the house means you're one of us, and stronger than you appear." Malena said.

We got back to Luke's studio, and Malena posed for him with her talisman, her knife.

I talked to her as she posed, and said, "So… about Dragon Guy… You two just like having fun together?"

Malena said, "Yeah! We make all these silly jokes, in between some great sex. I think it's the humor that really gets me, and he always tips me nice, too."

"I think that's a good human connection to have. He obviously doesn't think of you as just a whore, if he went out with you." I said.

"Oh, well that was just a friends thing. We already fuck for my job, and I… I don't want to jump into another Bram relationship again…" Malena said, "You warned me, but I still gave Bram another handy, and even a real eye. I should've taken both eyes out instead."

Luke said, "Maybe he'll appreciate having the extra peeper again, and put them somewhere they're supposed to be, like on his wife."

Malena said, "You're very optimistic, Luke. I like that."

I said, "He used to be a madman shouting in the streets, saying Jesus would come to kill us all."

Luke laughed, and said, "I had a different set of mindsets those days. I feel like I can actually think clearer, lately, and it's a breath of fresh air. I realized things aren't really so bad as they appear. Although I feel like I can do this picture better…"

I looked at it, and said, "Nah. It's great. I think you've really improved, actually. Everyone has different art styles, and your style is uniquely you."

Malena said, "Oh! Lemme see."

She looked at it, turned it at different angles, looking hard at it.

"How come it isn't doing anything? Like moving, or showing me hidden truths? You *are* magic, right? How could you not be, if you're dating the Devil's Daughter?" Malena said.

Luke looked at her quizzically, and said, "…I guess I'm not? I don't know, sometimes when you look at normal pictures hard enough they can seem to move. Is that what you mean?"

Malena looked at the picture for a long time, sitting on the bed and staring at it.

"My face looks different. I see it now. It's a trick, a perceptual sort of magic. I see it, though. My face expression changes, only to me, and because I'm looking at the picture differently." Malena said.

Luke said, "Exactly!! Y'know, that's why everyone says the Mona Lisa is smiling or frowning or not, because they're just looking at her weird smile in different lights, with their own perception."

Malena said, "I don't know. Seems like you could at least make it move its arms and legs or something."

Luke said, "...I can try to animate it? I've been trying my hand at that sort of thing, all stop motion-"

Malena said, "Nah, it's ok. Put this with the others, and come out with a grand playbook of us." and gave the picture back to Luke.

Malena

29

Francesca came back over, with Diane and Abbot. Francesca said, "I talked to this 'new woman,' our good friend, Diane, at the house, and I realized I forgot to thank you two for being my set of wheels as I was a third. It was really going well with that one guy, but as soon as our freak came out, he vanished. I have some chips if you guys want, and Diane brought some flowers for the pad."

Luke accepted the flowers graciously, as Diane smiled.

Luke said, "I know you don't want to do a pose, Diane… I don't know why, but I was going to ask, and then something told me I shouldn't. I still have to say that you're a beautiful woman, with beautiful flowers. I don't know why, but I have to say that."

I said, "Oh, she has that power. It's pretty cool and powerful and stuff. She's probably actually our strongest person at the house, besides the Madame."

Luke said, "No, I don't think it was anything forcing me to say that. I just felt like saying that."

Diane blushed, and said, "I can pose if you want."

Luke said, "You don't have to do anything that will intrude upon your comfort."

Diane smiled, and said, "Ok. I'll eat chips then and watch."

Abbot wiped off her tears, and said, "I want to do a real pose, now…"

"When you're crying?" Luke said, "That's ok if you want, but this will be a memorial of you- Oh."

Abbot waved a hand, and all the tears went away, and she was smiling sexily again.

"Got you all! I wasn't sad a bit!" Abbot said.

I just hugged her, and she hugged me back.

She posed, as we watched Luke draw.

"Very classy, Abbot." I said, "It's weird how you're the only one of us with no tattoos."

"I never wanted to scar my body with such hideous artwork that I will soon regret." Abbot said, "It's sacrilegious to the human form."

Luke said, "I can get that. I know other Christians who feel the same way. I've got one tattoo, one on my wrist to remember one of my near suicide experiences."

Diane asked, "What happened?"

"I flipped a coin on a cliff on a quarry, heads I would jump, tails I wouldn't. I got tails. I thought, eh, best two out of three, and flipped again. I got tails. I seriously thought something was fucking with me here, so flipped it again, one more time... and I got tails. I thought, ok, I said I wouldn't kill myself if I got tails, so I won't kill myself. I then shambled back to my car, in despair, because I *wanted to kill myself,* but didn't have any reason to, thinking that chance could choose for me. This is a real story, and I'm not making this up." Luke said.

Abbot said, "And then you realized that God saved you himself."

"Maybe. I don't know for certain. I just know I am very lucky. I have the back of the U.S. quarter on my wrist." Luke said, showing his tattoo, "I never knew what other tattoo I wanted to get, but this one is a good reminder for me, just that I am lucky, and that I can always live. I put it below my cutting scars, to remind me of that as well."

Diane said, "That's a very nice story. What happened that made you want to cut yourself?"

Luke said, "It was when I first started hearing voices, and it was a suicide attempt. I was scared of the voices, scared of what they said, and the only way out I thought to escape them was to die. That's a very twisted way to get out of something, but that's what I thought, as I was in constant, hellish torment hearing voices in my head telling me to kill myself."

Diane said, "So you listened to the voices?"

"In a way. But I tried to deny them, and in the end I did. I thought this was crazy, actually crazy, as I was bleeding out on the ground from the razor slashes, and then got up to get help. I collapsed before my father, hearing a static sort of noise, as his words were faint. I guess that's what blood loss can do to your mind." Luke said.

"I have many scars. But none are self inflicted. I keep them hidden." Diane said.

"I'm sorry, Diane." Luke said.

"It's ok. It is none of you people's fault. It is others'." Diane said.

Luke showed Abbot her picture, and she said, "Haha! I look even more better than all of you in this. Thank you, hottie." She went to give Luke a kiss, but then turned her head at the last second, and said, "Oh right, I've got a girlfriend now..." and looked at Tas entering the pad.

Affect

30

"I want to know your stance, Abbot. I want to know if you'll *actually* love me, like this. I couldn't get it out of my head, whether you were just casting an illusion like you do, or if you really love me. I want to know, now." Tas said.

"Well, I can blow you right now in front of all these people- Oh wait. That's right." Abbot said.

Tas frowned, and said, "I mean it, Abbot. I like being a woman, and I like women. I just need to know if you like me."

Abbot frowned too, now, and went up to Tas, and hugged her. Abbot whispered something in Tas's ear, and Tas broke down crying, as Abbot and Tas continued to hug.

She had said, "You are my soldier."

Tas and Abbot sat back, as Luke got them some beer, and Tas said, "My father wasn't a soldier. He was a mercenary. Basically criminal scum for hire. And I was his daughter- I mean, I was his son… at the time. He wanted me to be just like him.

"When he first saw me in a dress, he beat me.

"Shouting, 'You're a fucking *man!* Get it out of your head!! We kill, we fight, and we die, as *men!* Your mother was a slut, a no one who ditched me with you! Well I won't have some sissy for a son, who grows up to be some t girl *freak!*

"And now I am a t girl freak. I was a merc for a while, fighting with my father, and I always had a fantasy to be a soldier, but more the fantasy of just being a woman.

"I'm really so glad Diamond did this for me. But now based on what my penis said… I wonder if I should've just lived with it…"

I said, "Your penis was a dick. He sounded very unpleasant."

Tas wiped off her tears, and said, "That's correct. What are you all doing?"

Luke said, "I've got three poses with talismans down, and I'm wondering if you'd like to do the next?"

Tas said, "I don't have a talisman, though."

I said, "It's alright. Pose however you feel."

Tas smiled, and undressed for us. You couldn't even tell she had once been a man, actually. She was a gorgeous woman, with a lot of tattoos.

"Wow. Sexy artwork, Tas." Luke said, sketching her form.

"Thanks. I got kind of addicted to tats for a while. Is this cute enough?" Tas said.

"Yes. Actually… hold just like that. This will actually make a point, with this art. It will show that you're beautiful no matter what your genitalia." Luke said.

"Thank you for having that viewpoint. I was worried you'd actually be a misogynistic pig, sketching women just to jerk off to them later." Tas said.

Luke laughed, and said, "Nah, art doesn't really do that for me, even if it is the raunchiest I can think of. It's the feeling behind the art, which I am attracted to."

I smiled. That's what attracted me, too.

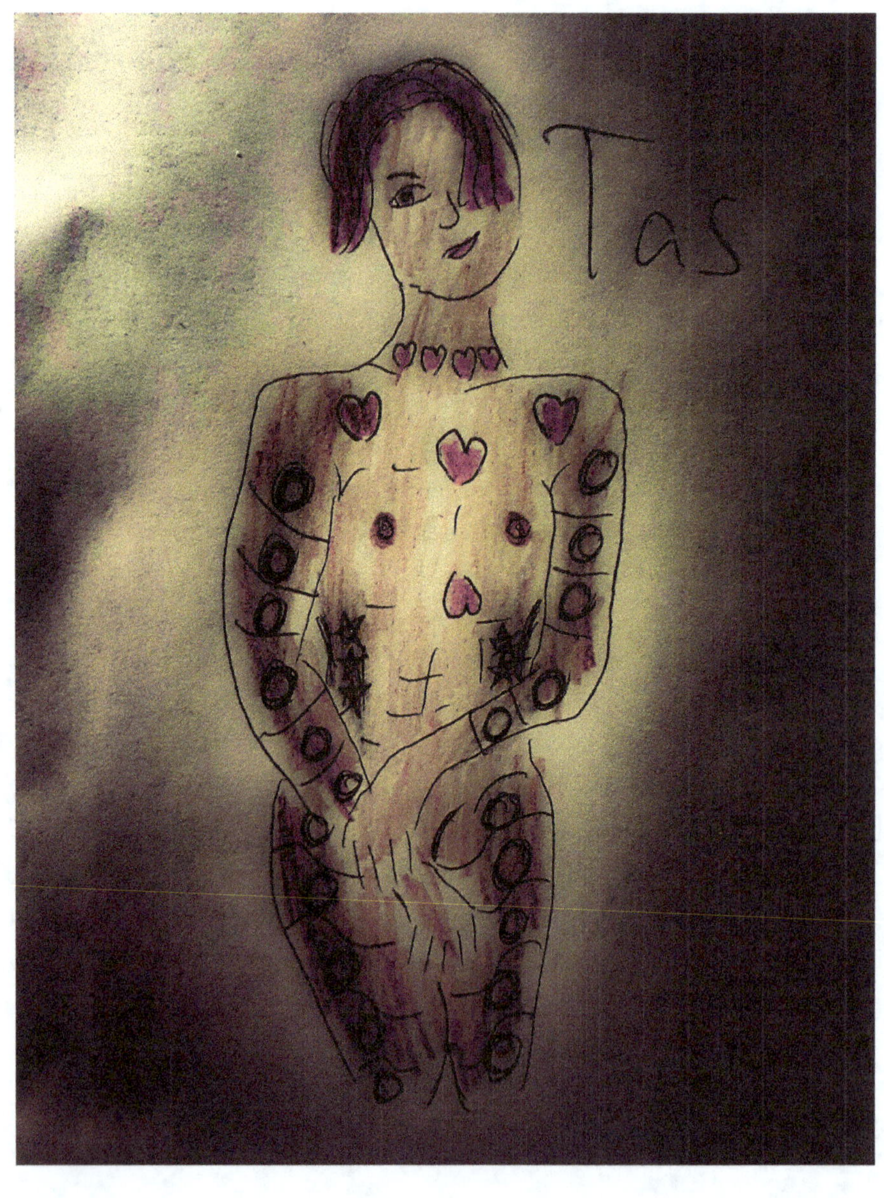
Tas

31

Diane said, "I know I declined. But I want to pose now. Completely without any illusion."

We were silent, as Diane took off her clothes, and then took off the illusion. We all gasped.

There were scars littering her form, even on her face, her breasts, everywhere.

Luke looked like he was going to cry, but continued to sketch.

"There are far too many scars even for memories. But the one over my eye was the first one. It happened when I said something by accident. I called my molester my father, even though I knew he wasn't.

"This one down by my privates is a painful memory to me. It is only because I tried to fight back, and they used force.

"The ones on my back was where I was whipped, like a common slave.

"I could go on, but I have made my point. I do not like to show this to most people.

"As you can see I am clutching a flower. That is my talisman. Wherever there is life, I have a talisman. It is in every plant, as they never ever have harmed me. If a plant is harming you, you are harming the plant, poison, barbs, whatever. It is only fighting back rightfully so.

"It was very painful in the asylum, without any sort of plant to protect me.

"But the Madame had a flower in her hat, and she gave it to me as she visited, scouting me out I assume.

"I could've used that flower to kill everyone in that asylum, as I desperately wanted to for so very long.

"But the Madame told me peace is more powerful than war, just like my plants. A plant does not kill needlessly. It may perhaps claim more territory than necessary, but if it does so it is only trying to live better.

"I walked out of those doors, in the Madame's arms, practically a babe again, free.

"I know you must think it odd that I worked as a prostitute after my past. But Tas has said it right, hasn't she, when it is difficult to teach an old whore new tricks.

"I had no education. I had no hirable skills. I actually didn't have my body, as none would sleep with someone so wretched as how I look right now.

"But the Madame offered me back my body, taught me ways to bring it back to life.

"I was much more hideous than how I look right now. I was starved, emaciated, filthy. The Madame bathed me, fed me, and protected me. And taught me magic to look however I desire.

"But I can still always see the scars, and I cannot ever get rid of them until I leave my body.

"You are all being very quiet. I am not using any magic on you. Why are you silent?"

I said, "I think you really are the strongest out of all of us. I am in awe."

Diane smiled at me, and said, "You have the power of life, Mary Jane. And you gave it to me as well when I wanted to snuff myself out. I think we are all powerful, in our own way, just as the Madame says."

"I did bring a chicken back to life, I guess. But how did all of our past troubles turn into that monster? I know I didn't do that, even though it says it's Abbot's dog. It frankly feels like a demon to me." I said.

"Ah yes." Diane said, "Your failure monster. Francesca told me about it. I believe that you know how it came to be, even though it may not be obvious. It leads a trail of sinister clues, straight back to its master."

"M-My father?" I asked.

"In a sense. This master serves your father, to serve itself. May I see your picture, Luke?" Diane said.

Luke wiped off his tears, and said, "I'm glad I could draw this. I didn't do you justice… but I hope it feels like life to you."

Diane smiled at the picture, and said, "It shows enough. Thank you, artist. You have power as well, even if you believe yourself mundane."

Diane

32

I posed last, as I was familiar in doing, with my artist. I held my talisman, Chuck, my princess wand.

"Great look, Jane. I'm loving the new tattoos." Luke said.

"Oh yeah, this heart one was with you in mind. You've got the key to my heart, babe." I said.

Luke smiled, and continued to draw.

Abbot said, "I've been kind of jealous of these two, actually. They seem to have this best friend boyfriend/girlfriend crap going on. That's not realistic at all!"

Francesca said, "Shush. They may say something interesting again."

Tas said, "Oh, quit it, you two. They just found true love and happiness, as you can tell by the symbols on Mary."

Malena said, "And dang, great bodies, too! That speaks for itself."

Diane said, "They are just making the most out of life with each other, in their tortured existence."

I said, "Well, all those things are true. I'm the Devil's Daughter, damnit. I deserve some true love and happiness, no matter how long we're going to keep this up."

Luke said, "And that you do… I think our first portfolio was pretty fun, don't you? This is neat branching out with other subjects."

"Ah, you just were obsessed with the demon girl, admit it." I said.

"I admit that. I was afraid and aroused, at the same time, my soul and body." Luke said.

Francesca said, "See! That sounded cool, both their stuff. Mary is so frank sometimes, and Luke puts an artistic take on things."

Abbot said, "You think they're gonna start doing it now? They're giving each other that look. I think I deserve to see some action, Mary, after you watched me do all my stuff."

I said, "Shush. If you turn invisible and try to pop in while we're doing it, I'll light you on fire."

Malena said, "Ahh... That sounds nice. Hot! So, Luke, you've had six different naked women in your studio, a once sex pad of Francesca's... What's going through your mind after all this, hmm?"

Luke said, "Honestly, it will be a blur of butts and boobs in my mind for a while, until I-"

I said, "Shh. Don't tell them that. It's our secret." and I winked at Luke as he blushed.

Tas said, "Goddamnit, I knew it. Well, whatever, I suppose if we've got some good pictures it will draw in the crowd. I wonder what the Madame will think of this."

Diane said, "I just let her know, and sent her some memories. She says she hates it, and would prefer if you all got naked at work instead of for some artsy lunatic she *knows* she'll have to buy a copy of his work just to get him off her back..."

I laughed, and said, "That's the Madame. Lemme see the pic."

I smiled to myself. Mary Jane. That's me, and how my artist sees me, a normal woman. Albeit holding a princess wand and trying to be taken seriously whilst doing so.

We all dispersed, well, they all dispersed, leaving Luke and I to kiss on the bed.

He looked very paranoid after a while, and stopped kissing.

He said, "They- He, just said I was being taken advantage of. I know that's wrong, because I had six lovely women naked before me. Sure doesn't feel like I'm being used. I want to destroy John's character, because it is like he is jamming a knife underneath my skin, into my brain."

"It's ok. And I hate them too. I hate my father, who's telling me to get off the bed." I said.

"I'm having an identity crisis, and I know I am me… but I don't know who they are, who you are, what is happening in my head. It is very confusing." Luke said.

"I feel like everyone is out to get me, to attack and beat me. I don't feel safe, even when I'm with you." I said.

We hugged, and tried to ignore the voices calling our names.

Eventually we played loud music to drown out the others. We had no neighbors, thank God, and we didn't really care too much.

We listened to the song, dancing in our rock and roll style.

We just danced, and drowned out the Hell in our minds.

This is why I love Luke. Because he is here, even in my Hell. And I am in Hell, even with him.

Even if it is just another day on Earth.

He roared a bestial roar, and I showed my demon form and cackled maniacally.

We continued to dance, hand in hand together.

Luke was dancing with the Devil's Daughter, and he used just the right amount of heat.

We felt each other's lust, my madman and I, and the Devil's Daughter seduced another victim into her bed.

The madman enjoyed the company.

We smoked cigarettes in the bed when we were through, then continued again for as long as we could.

I was sweaty, as the undead rooster crowed in the morning.

I said I had to get to work, and I felt the pang in my heart knowing I must leave my Luke for a while. He said he felt the same way.

I kissed him goodbye, and he said he'd be thinking of me. I said he'd be in my head too.

I practically could hear his voice, following me down the street, but I tried to ignore it as we each decided we wanted to keep telepathy to a minimum. It is a very disturbing magic, and never a good time, to one who hears other things in their head too.

I felt peace of mind, as I let all the voices pass again.

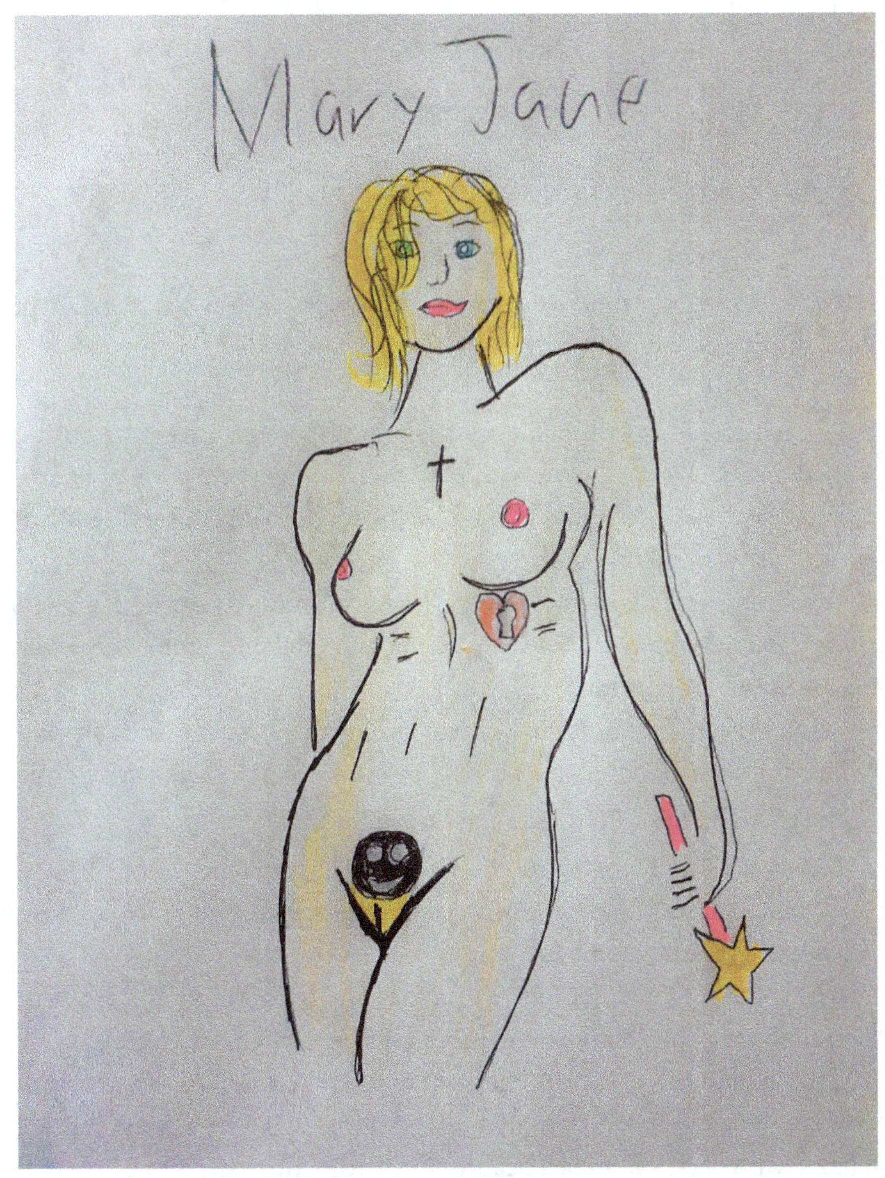
Mary Jane

33

I read Luke's journal, opening up to a page with a self portrait he made, before he left back to the States soon.

"I tried to kill myself again when Jane was gone. I tried to do it. I slashed myself over and over with the knife, on the same place as before.

I just had enough. I had enough fear, doubt, pain, misery, and torment. I just wanted it to end.

I was on the road down to Hell… I had committed suicide, a sin, and maybe I could rectify it in a few lifetimes in Hell and go to Purgatory, but for now I was damned.

Satan greeted me as a son, as I was completely on my guard. He said, *"What? I'm not omnipotent, omniscient, or any omni. I'm Satan, alike to you, and completely fallible. Relax, and then get on the rack."*

I spent a while being tortured by Satan, but someone found me after Satan went out for a smoke, giving me a brief respite and reveling in my fear for when he'd come back.

Mary Jane. She unlocked the binds, and said we could escape. I wanted to trust her, but I thought this must be some trick in Hell.

She told me about our time together, and said it was even better than Heaven. I accepted this compliment, and if this was a trick, I may as well enjoy it with such a familiar, beautiful face for a little while.

We snuck out of the house, as Cerberus was patrolling the fields of Satan's orchards, with sinners hanging from dead trees all around us. We snuck through the burning city, screams populating every corner, monsters stalking us, the damned howling in anguish. We got to the river, and Charon said, *"You're back? I shouldn't let you go. You both belong in Hell. Forever."*

Mary Jane said, "Aww, C'mon, Charon. You owe me. You were my first boyfriend, but were sooo boring, with your endless ferry trips."

Charon shrugged, and said, *"I thought it was nice, and you broke my heart, just as you will the living world when you escape again... But ok. As long as this doesn't become a trend."*

Charon took us across the river, as Jane held my hand, and I shivered from the cold, wounds still hurting from Satan's relentless onslaught.

We got to the steps, and Jane told me to run up them as fast as I could, that's how you avoid bad thoughts that keep you down in Hell. Just run.

We ran up those steps, my dead heart beating in fear.

It was endless, and as soon as I accepted that there actually would never be an end... the end approached. We got to the eternally sealed stone portal. Jane exclaimed, "Shit. There's no out anymore... Fucking Hell..." I pushed as hard as I could on the stone portal, as Jane sighed, saying, "I'll stay with you, Luke. We don't have to end just because we're stuck in eternal Hell-"

And as I was pushing the portal, praying, crying in anger, the stone portal moved.

It moved for me, just opened up, as if it allowed me to, and not because I pushed it.

We ran through the fields of limbo, I a ghost, and Jane said, "Yay! You can stay in my head forever-"

But an angel riding a pale horse came to meet us. She was... beautiful. She asked me if I would like to ride with her. All my heart wanted to accept this glorious angel, and her ride to Heaven.

I looked to Mary Jane, she sighed, crying, and said I could do whatever I wanted.

I hugged my Mary Jane, about to leave with my angel of death, but I couldn't escape her hug. She wasn't trapping me or anything... I just did not want to leave the hug.

The angel of death smiled, and said, "You can put off eternity for as long as you are living. I hope you had a good dream, artist, for you will wake up in regret for not accepting this ride. Be thankful for that, and the joy you will feel as well."

And I woke up, with no wound on my wrist, only the scars of the past. It was just a dream, but it felt so... real."

I smiled, and was glad I could heal the cuts from even such a far distance. I suppose the power of magic is enhanced for those you love.

I quickly put the journal back as Luke came out of the bathroom.

I asked him if he would be alright, back home again.

He said, "...I think so."

"You can stay here for a while, can't you? You *are* a Dutch citizen as well as American." I said.

"Yeah, but I didn't want to intrude on your thing." he said.

"Oh, believe me, it is not intrusion. I love that you're here, so stay for a while? Miss your ride up into the clouds again, for me?"

"Oh! Sure, I guess. It'll be kind of a setback for missing a return flight... but that sounds good, actually. I've been missing you to no end. I'm not really sure how to get any work done here, but maybe if I-" Luke said.

"I pitched the idea to the Madame, and you're going to be a sort of interview artist now. Just a little thing to get our stories down. We don't really have much to take back home, from our time here." I said.

"Ok. That sounds pretty fun, actually." Luke said, and smiled.

"Now... To start. When I left on the plane here, I felt such dread in my heart, knowing I was going to accept my true potential..." I said.

Self
There was a time when the world was good. It can be good again.
There is always a reason to live.
but she smiled at me, and my heart fast
Happiness is a struggl

34

Tas and Luke got along pretty well. I guess it was something about language for them, or perhaps because they were both mundane, or maybe Luke just liked her tattoos.

They laughed in the pad, as Tas whispered in his ear. Tas slapped him on the knee, making Luke jump, and Tas smiled and waved goodbye to us, going back to her own home.

I said, "...You get turned on by Tas!"

Luke tried to hide his arousal, and said, "Is that wrong? I'd hate to think that I like her only because she was once a man, but I think it's cool that she knows, like, what it's like to be one as well! You don't find that sort of understanding all the time, in the female race."

"Pfft. She's cute, attractive, a tough girl... and I can see why anyone would like her. Her and Abbot are already doing it nonstop, so don't get your hopes up, babe. That spot is filled by a woman." I said, smiling.

"I guess that's true. Kind of a bummer, eh?" Luke said and grinned.

I pushed him on the bed, and unbuckled his belt.

When I took off his pants he, gasped in terror.

I had turned his genitalia into that of a woman's, an illusion, but a realistic one.

"Wh-What-" he said.

"Shh… We're going to do a little role reversal, just so you know how Tas feels." I said.

I waved my wand, and made Luke turn into a full female illusion.

He felt himself, couldn't stop feeling himself, but stopped as I pulled down my own pants.

"…Shit." he said.

I grinned, and began fucking my boyfriend, now female, like a man does, although a nice, gentle, generous man.

He blushed when we were finished, after moaning for sooo long together.

I waved my wand, let him perceive himself and me as we were again, and he said, "…Ok. That was… an experience. I think I never want to do that again, actually. Even though it was… well, I've never felt that way in all my life."

I smoked a cigarette, still feeling him clutching my back as I boned the bejesus out of him, and said, "Get used to it, because if you ever cheat on me for Tas, I'm gonna do that to you every night."

"…Ok. Point taken." Luke said.

I kissed him on the cheek, and said, "You were taken by a woman who turned herself into a man briefly. It's not always the best feeling, knowing you're not the one calling the shots."

"So… Why did Tas… want to give up that 'power?'"

"Who knows. Maybe it's a deep identification of being someone you always wanted to be. I never said that Tas gave up that power… In fact, women can be the tops, the doms, the powerhouses, anytime they like. A lot of the time the man doesn't understand this, and it gives unsatisfying, unequal sexual relations. Some people like being in charge, and some like being taken charge of… But I prefer equality, don't you?" I said.

"Hell yes. It's waaay more fun, in my opinion." Luke said.

"And that's why I showed you how to get off like a girl. Now. I want you to do that to me, with female parts, just so you can reclaim your power, and realize that we trade off every few seconds in our relationship. Most of the time we are working together, to give each other absolutely what the other wants, which is what we want. I like that in our relationship." I said, and waved my wand again, and got on my back.

Luke the lady looked nervous, but I told him to go wild.

Ahh…

We sat back, after putting our clothes on, and I turned Luke back, and Luke said, "So that's really a lesbian relationship, huh?"

"In a sense. You'll probably never know what it's like to feel it for real. You're actually the first 'woman' I've slept with! I thought it was a fun time, didn't you?" I said.

"…Yes. But… let's keep this to ourselves, shall we?" Luke said.

I kissed him on the cheek, and said, "That's a man's pride for you. Hold onto that, and be proud of it as well, because not every man wants to have to live up to that, which is absolutely ok."

"Hmm… Ok. Thank you for this experience, Jane." Luke said.

35

Luke said, as we were drinking coffee at a cafe, "I want to confess that I find you and all of your friends attractive, in different ways. You being my first choice, but the choice that honestly I never thought I could achieve, the last one on the list probably being my first actual possibility..."

"Did you rate me and my friends?? Ok, you weirdo, give me the order." I said.

"You, Tas, Diane, Francesca, Abbot, Malena... Sorry." he said.

I burst out laughing, and said, "You think you could get with Malena so easily?"

"...I guess not. We kind of came to an understanding, it's her job to please, and not her job to please me. Although she's the one I am most comfortable with, not counting you." Luke said, sipping his coffee.

"She's comfortable with everyone, though." I said.

"I know. That's why we get along so well." Luke said.

"...Hm. Ok. Then... Abbot... I think it was just a front, her whole flirting with you thing. She's kind of an underhanded bitch." I said.

"You know everyone falls for the maneaters, even if we know the illusion. It's a pretty hot act, and I can see Abbot uses it well in life." Luke said.

"Is that why you two get along? Because you know each other's illusions?" I asked.

"No, I just get those kinds of ladies. Every man *wants* to get those kinds of ladies, because even if you know she's a backstabbing bitch, she's *your* backstabbing bitch. I think Abbot knows I don't think of her as that way really, so puts down the barrier and shows real kindness and love." Luke said.

"She did that to me, too, but was just in rival bitch mode at the start, and not hot maneater mode." I said, "I can see how everyone likes Francesca. She's smart, sexy too, even though she hides behind her work."

"She's kind of a difficult case. I feel like I would never measure up to her, in terms of work. But, she's not all her job, and really shows the woman inside, the attractiveness of humanity, in her natural demeanor. She's also got a cool hold at art, and that's a plus for me." Luke said.

"Yeah… I hope she meets someone nice soon." I said.

"She's intimidating, without a doubt, but I think eventually she'll find someone who's not scared of her power, mundane or magical." Luke said.

"And Diane?" I asked.

"I want to protect her. That is all. She doesn't need my protection, and I respect that." Luke said.

"And so we get to your favorite girly… Tas." I said, sipping my coffee.

Luke shrugged, and said, "Tats, dialogue, something incredibly new and mysterious, a soldier, a smart mouth, a gorgeous figure… She's definitely second on my list, even though she was a man. I never knew I could like someone like that, and maybe that's a turn on in itself."

"And so, with all these lovely possibilities… you're stuck with me. Why's that?" I said.

"You have the hottest body, hotter than Hell, from Hell, you are the coolest, the smartest, the strongest. I'm not making this up to flatter you.

This is how I see you. You also show struggle, mental or not, and that feels relatable to me. You've been in the worst, and can help me through the worst. I've never felt better than being with you, and you really make me feel happy." Luke said.

I blushed, and said, "I want to reject those compliments, I want to show my demon form, and have you run away in fear... but that only drew you closer, and I am thankful for that."

"You're *not* the worst. You're the absolute best." Luke said.

"Thanks, Luke. Now I want to tell you how I see you. You're a nutjob, for real, and that is the best thing about you, honestly. You look good, in a way I can't describe, that is very pleasing to me. You're a bit of a weirdo, but who isn't at heart? It makes me feel accepted. You are incredibly adept at mundane magic, words and art, even if you believe yourself to be only adequate. You have a hard time saying I love you, but that is only because you have been hurt in the past. I love you, Luke, and I want you to know that." I said.

"...I love you too, Mary Jane." Luke said.

"And you said it, even without saying that very common phrase. You said it with our entire conversation, much more in depth than simple repetition of 'I love you.' I do like saying it, though." I said.

"I guess. Let's keep it to when it counts, and-" Luke said.

"I love you, I love you, *I love you.* Take that." I said, and smiled, holding his hands.

"I love you too." Luke said, and smiled.

We kept on saying it, walking back to the pad, we were trying to get the words out of our system, but instead of getting boring, it just got more fun to say it.

I had the words stuck in my head, as I went back to the house, and I fell asleep later in the night with them in repetition.

I love you.

36

I skipped the Madame's lesson on telepathy. I knew that would only be disturbing to me, and with my pills it would make it difficult besides, so went to see if Diamond could teach me anything.

She taught me how to summon eidolons.

"Many eidolons are not real souls, but the fractured and unfractured feelings, emotions, and discarded fancies of mortals. You yourself... erhem... could be identified as one of these." Diamond said.

"What? What do you mean?" I asked.

"I would have to show you what is beneath existence for you to understand correctly, and that might make you go insane, so we'll save that for another day. You were created by an angelic soul, Lucifer, and your mother, a normal human." Diamond said.

"Yes... I *am* the Daughter of the Devil and Mary..." I said.

"Correct. I will show you how to summon one of them, or at least your conjoined feelings of them, into a form you choose. They will not be actual souls, and I believe an actual soul is tethered much more to their previous body, so we will use the element you are in tune with to bind them. Fire." Diamond said.

"Oh. So it's gonna be, what, a fire creature?" I asked.

"More or less. Concentrate on what you feel of your mother, what you believe of her, or your father if you prefer..." Diamond said.

"...Let's do my mother. Then what? I really don't know that much about her, actually... I just know that I miss her, even though I never knew her." I said.

"Perfect. Anchor those feelings, tie them down, and burn bright, a small flame at the start." Diamond said.

I concentrated... and lit a flame with Chuck. It grew, a tongue of fire on the star... and I just put all my shame, anger, depression, and feelings of love tied to my mother into that flame.

I remembered seeing her corpse, after she took her own life.

The flame ruptured into a blaze, streaming out of the wand, and soon a claw was grabbing out of the flame, trying to reach at me.

I stepped back, but I was holding the flame with my wand, so could not escape.

"Excellent. Now let this form come forth into the world." Diamond said.

I looked at the eidolon, and I saw the dead face I had seen before.

"N-No, I don't want to see this form of my mother. I don't want to have this exist." I said.

"And yet she does. Quick, bind this eidolon with its name." Diamond said.

I did not want to call this thing Mary, or my mother, or anything at all.

I swore, "Hell!!" as it touched my hand, and the searing fire actually hurt me, like it never did.

The grasping claw turned into a loving touch, even though it still hurt.

And Diamond said, "Congratulations. You have bound Hell itself. Your guardian eidolon will ever be at your back, and watch over you, for it is Hell."

"N-No. I don't want this." I said.

Diamond laughed gently, and said, "You were always meant to be the ruler of Hell, Devil's Daughter."

I looked at Diamond. I saw millions of demons at her back, ones I never saw before. They were whispering to her, telling her what to do...

She simply chatted politely back to them, and took their counsel, accepting or rejecting ideas.

"Y-You're a monster." I said to Diamond, as I was holding back Hell.

"I was coal... but I was forged in pressure and heat, and now I am Diamond. I await your command, our lady, as does the entirety of HELL." Diamond said, kneeling before me.

I tried to rip her apart with Hell, and she accepted this verdict.

And she laughed in fire, disappearing in smoke and ash.

All that was left was a silver looking, actually common steel, scalpel.

She was added to Hell.

She whispered in my ear, *"Take my scalpel. Take my power, and command me as your slave. You can be the master of your nightmares, and you won't fail..."*

I said, "You made the failure monster. You brought that spirit to life."

"I did. I cut off Tas's penis, I found the eye in the trash, as well as the dummy. I counseled Abbot on her dog, and she always knew the truth, but did not admit it to my face... And I brought your failure to life. I could not bring a real soul, but eidolons are far more agreeable, are they not? Only you have the power to bring real souls to life, as you did your rooster." Diamond said.

"I will not accept your power!! I will not accept Hell!!" I yelled, holding back the spirit.

"So be it. I was always Hell, in the end, and I will always be Hell. But like deep in the Earth, deep in Hell... you can find a Diamond.

"I will await you, with our master, if you do not become the master." Hell said.

And pop, the spirit put itself out, and I was holding Chuck... alone, with a scalpel and ashes on the floor.

I looked at the scalpel, picked it up... and sighed, pocketing it.

37

Abbot said, "...Is that even a shirt? Can you even... wear that?"

I said, "It's my day off, so I can wear whatever I want. It was my very first shirt."

"Hm. Yeah, I meant if that will actually stay on your body. It looks like rags." Abbot said.

I sat on her bed, and we gossiped for a bit. It's been so long since I actually *could* have girl talk that wasn't veiled threats and bitchiness. We got onto a subject of Tas, and Abbot said, "She makes me so frustrated!! She *always* does that! You know, that one thing!"

"Oh, I know. Luke does this one thing, y'know, the one thing, and it drives me bonkers! I wish they'd just take our hints." I said.

Abbot sighed, and said, "I guess you can take the dick off the man, but you can't take the dick out of the man. Oh well. So now that you killed our nurse, what are we gonna do when one of us gets some STD again? I mean, Malena can maybe cure it, but it's a perk for customers not to wear a condom, and it was our secret edge over the competition. Was Diamond really some sort of demon?"

"She was just a very, very disturbed individual... The scalpel tells me secrets, past horrors that it had done under her hand. I don't like to think of it, or listen to it, but I don't know what will happen if I throw it out. Probably end up killing someone by accident, it's so evil. I think you should just bite the bullet and practice safe sex, just in case." I said.

Abbot rolled her eyes, and said, "You're so mundane, yet so not. I don't know how some child of Hell could be so normal, even preaching safe sex. And anyway, how come you get an off day cuz you killed someone?? Fuck, I'd kill you all if I could get off my back for a week or so."

"Why can't you just make your own hours? Shouldn't that be a thing, since you do all your own work? And the Madame wanted me rested and protected, in case of some sort of 'ultimate crisis' I could go through." I said.

"I guess I do other things around the house as well... But I *did* think about starting up on my own, just get a booth or two, maybe with Malena if she was into it, but it's very tough to swim on your own in this job. We've got Tas hooking us up with anyone she can, we've got Francesca keeping us out of the government's eyes, and the *competition...* God, you think I'm a bitch? Wait 'til you get *them* spreading nasty rumors about you every which way just to get you out of the water." Abbot said.

"I don't know, it doesn't matter to the normal, dumb tourist which whore they go to, as long as they're pretty. I guess the Madame does offer her workers some protection, and man, it sure would be difficult to find any other teacher in magic." I said.

"Exactly. We're fucking gods on this street, just because we have the Madame on our side. Can I try to exorcise the scalpel?" Abbot said.

"What? You can do that?" I said.

"Mhm. I practice the magic of God, silly, of course I can exorcise something. Dad taught me himself." Abbot said.

"A whore is exorcising a demonic scalpel. Huh. I guess that does sound pretty magical." I said, as Abbot got off the bed, and led me with her to a holy place.

She took me to a very special, unused room. I always passed by this room, although dusted it occasionally, because it was never used.

"This was the spot that a saint lost her virginity." Abbot said.

"Oooh. Sounds naughty. Who was this saint?" I asked.

"Y'know, Saint? The one working girl down by the canal? She felt Jesus in her bed, in this very room, and he blessed her with the best twat in the entire world. She could retire with all the cash she makes, but she donates it every day to parishes, and only keeps what she needs to live, the bare minimum. That's why she's called Saint." Abbot said, "She used to work with us, but decided to accept her calling and spread the Lord's will on her own, with everyone she can, and not be exclusively ours."

'...This doesn't sound like normal doctrine. Are you sure that was really Jesus?" I said.

"Nobody knows, but that's what Saint says. The Lord works in mysterious ways. And I believe her, just because... I saw it." Abbot said.

"What?? Really? What did Jesus look like to you? I've seen God, but only in a dream." I said.

"I was blinded by beauty. Really. There were bright lights and this sort of *heavenly* aura around the room. And y'know what's the kicker? Jesus used a condom, and after Saint was done moaning in absolute, orgasmic bliss, it popped out of her, and Jesus left the room. I never saw his face, he was so classy, but I knew just by a feeling that he was there, looking at Saint so absolutely, extremely fulfilled." Abbot said.

"...Are you making this up?" I asked.

"I swear to- I mean, I won't take the Lord's name in vain, especially not *here.* Put the scalpel on the bed, and we'll see if Jesus can lend us a hand." Abbot said.

I placed the scalpel on the bed.

Abbot said, "By *Jesus Christ! Begone, demon, and leave this holy house!!*"

The scalpel did nothing.

"Well, I tried. Oh well." Abbot said.

"...That was all?" I said.

"Fuck, I don't know any of the actual incantations. It's all old Latin and shit. That's what my dad said before to a demon, and it left." Abbot said.

"What demon?" I asked.

"Oh, just one of my old boyfriends. My dad was visiting, and he *really* didn't like that guy." Abbot said.

"...Oh well. I guess it's just a cursed scalpel then." I said, picking up the scalpel.

The scalpel whispered to me, *"Hell awaits, Mary Jane."*

I ignored it, and put it back in my pocket.

I walked out with Abbot, and we got our phones back today, and Tas was calling her dad. She said to him, "I really did it, Dad. I know, you hate me now, and we don't have to talk anymore-"

Her dad said, as I listened passing by, "I'll come visit soon, I swear. I mean it this time. I love you, Tashan."

"I love you too, Dad." Tas said.

38

I watched as an old bum, a hitchhiker, a traveler, and once merc, Tas's dad, hit on Abbot at the house.

Tas said, "...Um, Dad... You're really trying too hard-"

"I knew my guy liked girls still!! It's ok if you're a girl, really, as long as you like girls!! That's right, right? I don't know, Tashan... I am having a very difficult time of this." Tas's father said.

Tas took her dad's hand, as her dad cringed at the touch, and Tas said, "Really, Dad. I know you have a lot of judgement about me, about my work and things too, but it is ok. I can accept it, and I will tell you how I feel about it too."

Tas's father said, "...I think it's great you're... working... as something! You don't- You don't do girl's things here, do you??"

Tas smiled, and said, "I'm more the middleman, Dad."

Tas's dad sighed in relief, and said, "Thank God. I- I- I don't think I would be able to see you degrade yourself, like your mother, and be happy with it..."

Tas shrugged, and said, "You fucked a filthy whore, and you got me. What's wrong with helping other women like my mother?"

"...Nothing. It's just... Nothing is wrong with it. I have complete and total acceptance. That's what the U.S. people are fond of saying, right? Acceptance? It's been so long since I've been there..." Tas's father said.

Tas saw me, and waved me over. Tas said, "This is Mary Jane, and she's from the U.S. Maybe she can tell you about how everything changed-"

Tas's dad immediately started putting the moves on me.

Tas said, "...She's the maid, Dad."

"Hot! Are they all different sorts of sexy characters like maids, princesses, and sacrificial virgins? I do believe I need to visit your work more often!" Tas's dad said.

Tas said, "...No. She's just the maid. And you're broke, Dad... I can't really get one of the girls to do something for free like that."

"...You can't? I thought you had more clout." Tas's dad said.

"Sorry, Dad. I'm not the one in charge, I'm just the middleman. The one in charge is the Madame." Tas said.

"...Is she a sexy character too?" Tas's dad said.

"No, she's a very old practitioner of magic. But I'll let you meet her yourself." Tas said, and took her dad down the hall.

Abbot sighed out, and said, "It's nice meeting my girlfriend's father... but still... I hate trying to act polite to bums."

"Ah, get over it. He could be your father in law, one day." I said, grinning.

"...Shut it. I think that's the meanest thing you've ever said to me, having to be that man's daughter in law... He immediately went into a very detailed metaphor of him fucking me, in an impolite manner, with blatant disrespect to women, in front of his daughter who is now a woman. I think I would hurl, having to even just shake hands with him at a wedding with Tas." Abbot said.

"So you really are dreaming of a wedding, eh?" I said.

Abbot blushed, and said, "No! Why did you assume that?? Cut it out, because you're just as bad as the rest of this displaced American trash, even if you're from Hell."

I shrugged, and said, "Comes with being a bum. You gotta live life while you can. I was homeless for a long time after I got out of Hell, until I seduced and deceived my way to adequate power."

"Degeneracy. Disgusting. Disturbing. I don't know about any of Tas's family... but I love her, if anything. I haven't told her that, do you think I should??" Abbot said desperately.

"Why not. If Tas is happy with it, you'll both be happy, right?" I said.

"...Good point! I'm very new to being in love, although trying *hard* at it for very long. I thought I'd have to give up prostitution to actually find love, but Tas... Tas knows it's work. I know she gets jealous sometimes, but really... No one, and I mean no one, does what we do in the bed, because I don't even take any other females to bed with me anymore, and if I did they wouldn't enjoy it as much as I enjoy Tas. It's like... a secret, a lovely secret, of ours, that I can indulge in and explore with, that my partner enjoys as well." Abbot said.

"I'm glad for you. That really makes me feel happy. Despite you being Nederlander whore trash." I said.

"We're all trash together." Abbot said, and punched me on the arm.

Tas's dad came back, blinking his eyes a bunch.

Tas said, "Are you ok, Dad?"

Tas's dad said, "I think... That was no sacrificial virgin. She... I think I need to sit down. I am very happy that you have found your calling, Tashan, in life, love, and work. And your body. I'm happy you can be you."

Tas smiled, and said, "Aww. Thanks, Dad. I knew the Madame would change your mind."

Tas's dad sighed, and gave Tas a hug.

Tas's dad started crying, and said, "Y-You... You are my only son-daughter... and I am so proud of you. I love you, Tashan."

Tas hugged him back, said, "I love you too, Dad." and they were both soon crying together.

Then Abbot hugged with them, saying, "I love you too, Tas!!"

They all just hugged together, as I watched.

39

Malena and I went to visit Diane at her flower stand. We looked at all the flowers, and Malena grabbed a big armful and smelled them. "Beautiful. Absolutely beautiful, Diane." Malena said.

Diane said, "Thank you. I only buy from sellers who I know treat their workers well, or out of the way independent growers. Both of you may take one, in thanks for coming to visit me... It's been rather lonely sometimes."

I said, "I think this is a much better career choice for you. We've got your back, and from what you've told me you've saved up quite a bit! You should be able to do fine in the flower business, even if it doesn't take off astronomically."

Malena said, "I wanted to ask you... Diane... How you feel about me, because of when we performed as Sinbad and Diane, the Star Crossed Lovers... I never realized how much you hated being... well, having someone insert something into you."

"You were by far the best one, Malena." Diane said, "And if you re- member correctly, I asked you as Sinbad first if he would like to perform with me. It was completely my choice, and if you refused you wouldn't have even remembered the question."

Malena said, "You didn't even recognize me at first, which I was surprised at."

"You have remarkable talent in your body." Diane said, "You could be anyone you want, at any time, and still make them feel like they are a brand new, unique individual."

Malena smiled, and said, "I can. You were very nice when you asked, and I kinda thought you were flirting with me. I know, that's silly."

Diane said, "Of course it is not. If I wanted to flirt with you, you would remember it... So do you remember it?"

Malena smiled, and said, "That I do."

I could practically feel the love, kindness, and goodwill going on between these two. I hazarded to hook them up with each other.

"Um... So, what if us three got drinks-" I said.

Malena said, looking at me, "Not gonna happen, Mary. I'm like Diane's big sister, and the Star Crossed Lovers thing was only an act. Thank you for trying, but I'm going with Dragon Guy to a movie, later this night."

Diane said, "Oh, and I am seeing someone as well. You'd be surprised at how attractive the tulip seller is. It actually would've been a good act for a show, and you guys should contemplate it sometime."

Malena and I both said, "You are??"

"He's a very unique individual, even though he feels like a failure. He spotted me immediately as someone special and important. His friends are fun, always there for him, and he really makes me feel safe. If anyone knows what it's like to be locked up, used like a doll, and suffocating in a box, it is him." Diane said.

I said, "...This person sounds kind of familiar."

Diane said, "I wouldn't worry about it. Even though he has a new penis, I can tell from his demeanor, from reading his very mind and spirit, that he would never use it on someone to cause pain."

I said, "...Um... Ok. I- I- I guess I'll take... this black tulip? I guess it's cool you got it to be black. Is it paint?"

Diane said, "Some flowers grow in the nether regions, in the very abyss, and the flower you chose did just that. I think it will suit you well. Wear it for some special occasion."

Diane then handed me the black tulip, and I accepted it.

I went out with Luke, Malena, and the Dragon Guy to a movie, and I wore my tulip in my hair.

There was a special on old, old films, so we watched Frankenstein.

I thought of my rooster and our failure monster. Did these monsters just want to be loved as well?

Should I accept this failure, learn from it, and even keep it close to my heart, so that I may never commit the same one?

I looked at Frankenstein's monster going, "RAA! RAA!" and shambling about in that stiff posture.

Our monsters were actually quite... I would almost say they were human, for if there is anything most human about us, it is anger towards our creators, and their failures.

Diane walked in late to the movie, with our failure monster. They didn't notice us, and weren't expecting us.

They sat politely with each other, holding hands.

The undead rooster on our monster's shoulder cockadoodle dooed as the movie ended, and we clapped for the show.

40

Luke came into the house, for a strange reason. He said he needed my help.

"...Um... Jane... There's someone who has invaded my studio, and for all the life of me I don't know how to get rid of him. He just barged in like he owned the place, and claims he's lived there all his life..." Luke said, catching me on my break.

I sighed, and said, "Lemme guess. Mister Monster..."

Luke said, "I named him John. Seemed like an adequate name."

"...Is John acting polite?" I asked.

"He's the rudest, loudest, most annoying roommate I've ever had, but I think that's why we get each other. I just wanted to know... Is it ok that he stays with me?" Luke said.

I stared at him, but couldn't stop the smile that was appearing on my face.

I said, after the smile had completely appeared, "Thank you for accepting our failure."

"Oh, John and I just think it's stupid that he got all freakish on you guys. He actually feels kind of bad for it. He doesn't really know how to apologize, and really doesn't want to actually, but maybe we can get together sometime and all have lunch." Luke said.

"Ok. Let's get this over with, then. We can go now." I said, taking off my smock.

"...Now??" Luke said.

"No time like the present! I'll round up the girls. Go get John, and find somewhere public with a lot of people just in case he goes wild. I don't want him terrorizing anyone if things go south." I said.

I informed the Madame, in her telepathy way, just that I needed to confront this.

She said...

Be careful, and realize that overcoming our failures can be the greatest victories of our lives.

I went with Abbot, Francesca, Malena, Tas, and Diane, meeting Luke and John at a brunch place.

John was saying to Luke, "Why don't you just kill yourself already? Cockadoodle doo, dummy, you're a moron, and no one loves you."

Luke said, "I think you have to realize the more you push, the more I feel like living, actually. You're a real dick, John."

John said, "I have a dick, I am a dick, I am dick. I also have a cock on my shoulder, so deal with it."

The undead rooster crowed, and we sat at the table as Luke waved to us and John ignored us.

John turned his head from pouting away from us, and looked at Diane. John said, "I'm sorry you have to see this shitshow, babe."

Diane said, "We are all shit, and this is the show. Now let us all be adults and make peace, for the betterment of our lives."

John huffed, and said, "I think they should say sorry first."

I said, "So you really do want to say sorry for being such a dick? Rooster, you killed some people, and that is totally not cool."

The undead rooster made chicken noises in John's ear, and John said, "You would do the same if someone tried to kill you."

I said, "But he's dead! He's supposed to be dead!"

John said, "Well, we both know you fucked that up, so fucking deal with it, you hoe."

Luke said, "Don't talk to her that way, or I'm going to seriously hurt you, no matter if you're a dummy."

Francesca said, "Yeah!! You're a fucking dummy!! Why... are you *such* an asshole?? I thought we were having the best relationship of our lives!!"

John said, "It's weird what having no voice can do in a relationship. You basically raped me, every day. It was impossible to say no."

Francesca said, "You couldn't even think it!! I do not understand you."

John huffed, and said, "Well, care for me to fuck you for real, then? I'll do everything you did to me to you, even shove my fingers up your ass to make you vibrate... Would you like that?? I know I didn't."

Diane said, "It is ok, John. You have no need to make empty threats."

John frowned, and said, "For you it would be an empty threat. For these bitches I'd fucking do everything that happened to you to them, just to make some sort of rectification."

Diane said, "That is very sweet, but these people are not my tormentors, and I believe they are not yours as well."

Abbot stuttered, "H-How can I ever say sorry to you? I feel awful even thinking that you d-died that way."

John rolled his eyes, and said, "If it makes any difference, there's no way I am actually a dead puppy dog. I mean, look at me. I look like a little hound to you? If I am, I sure am not now. All I know is that I know how it felt to die that way, who knows if it really happened to 'me.'"

Malena said, "Then what you said about Bram wasn't real as well?"

"Oh no. That was totally true. I checked up on him, and he's having the time of his life, getting a promotion, getting things back together with his wife... all because of the confidence you gave him from giving his eye back. But still. He wants to come down and get a 'normal' handy like he used to. I'm glad the dick I got isn't his anymore." John said.

Tas said, "...I want to say, I really feel that I am in a better spot as I am, and no matter what, I do not want you back."

John said, "I'm fucking fine with that. Most people would fucking kill themselves if their dick was chopped off, but you... Well, I guess you're stronger than most men."

Tas smiled, and said, "Thank you, penis. I am a woman, and I have always been proud of that."

John said, "See, why can't you all be like the t girl and fucking own up to your mistakes. I'm *not* fucking sorry for being a dick, for getting a handy when my life is shit, for being a dummy, being abused by a little girl, and having a good, normal, undead friend."

I sighed, and said, "I guess that's life, and I own up to giving you that life, rooster."

"Oh, fuck off. You think you're *sooo-*" John said.

The rooster hopped onto the table, walked over to me, and sat on my lap.

John said, "...Ok. Alright, if he's cool with you, that's cool with me. I *listen* to my friends, unlike some of you."

Francesca said, "...You were really my best friend, and if I could've listened to you, I would've."

John rubbed his eyes, sighing, and said, "I mean, I guess you are my creator, too. I never really thanked you for that, because you created me just to get off. You took no responsibility in your creations, Francesca, Jane."

I stroked the undead rooster, who seemed very happy with it, and Francesca said, "I just wanted a companion. I thought I could build a replica of that, even though I never thought I would actually succeed. I would like to be your friend, if that is possible, and we don't need to be at each other's throats. I will never do what I did to you ever again. Besides having our lonely meals together... I think that was acceptable."

John said, "Fuck, if you're paying, why the fuck not."

Malena said, "...So, John... I mean... Are you saying I should get back together with Bram? Since I changed his life?"

John smacked his forehead, and said, "God. You are really fucking stupid. How can you be, like, the best in the sack, know what is going on with people with just a touch, and still be so stupid. I do not love you. Get that in your head. Read my lips. I do not love you. Bram is married, and even his old glass eye has an eye on someone else."

Malena said, "...Ok. I was just checking. I don't love you, either. I hoped I could, but now I know that will never be. Thank you for giving me closure."

John stared at her, and said, "You're smarter than you look, that's for sure."

Diane said, "And that wasn't so bad, was it? You all have said sorry, and we are at peace. Let us order now, because it would be a shame to waste such good company."

Abbot said, "I've always loved you, and you were my best friend. I'm sorry."

John sighed, and said, "I'm sorry too, Abbot, and it's not your fault. I'll get the check. I have practically an inexhaustible body thanks to Francesca, and I've been working nonstop lately. Luke, this fucking idiot, gave me a place to stay purely out of the kindness of his heart, even though when I knocked on the door he threatened to kill me. I guess you're all not so bad, in your own ways."

We all ate together, talking at brunch, and I fed my failure, my good friend the rooster, muffin bits as he sat on my lap.

41

My abyssal, dark flower wouldn't die, apparently. It's been a week already since I got it from Diane, and it still looked so… vibrant, despite being black.

We hugged and kissed Diane goodbye, shaking hands with John. The two got a Ford 69, what John always wanted, and decided to tour the continent spreading love, joy, and flowers.

We all knew, without really knowing exactly how, that Diane could protect herself, even over having a monster man and an undead rooster at her side. She said to me after I asked if she really would be ok, "I could be the ruler of the world, if I decided to, and you all would choose me as one unanimously. I know this, and now you know this too. It is not my place to grasp at such petty power… I believe true power comes in slighter ways, like sunshine after a rainy day, or finding nice people when you do not believe a single one exists."

"I knew that you were the Queen of Holland, babe." John said to her.

Diane said, "Queen of Russia, Queen of Egypt… all the others, and more. It is getting late, we should get to our first campsite! I am so very excited."

I hugged her one more time, and we waved them goodbye, as they walked out of the doors of the house. The rooster cockadoodle dooed at me, in its horrible way, which actually kind of grew on me.

And strangely… I felt the rooster's soul leave my own body.

The rooster fell off John's shoulder, and John looked at it, and burst out crying, kneeling on the floor and cradling the rooster.

I fell to the floor as well.

The rooster looked at me before Heaven's gates.

I pet him, how he was, looking like a living rooster. He looked into my eyes with both eyes there, an everlasting rooster's soul.

I hugged him goodbye, and saw someone approach from behind him.

I looked up, and I gasped.

There was my mother, Mary, smiling gently at me.

I burst out crying, and she wiped off the tears with the back of her hand.

She hugged me goodbye, and took the rooster with her back through the gates of Heaven.

I woke up, in relief.

I always assumed that she must've gone to Hell, for killing herself, for having sex with the Devil.

But she was in Heaven.

I just felt so much joy and happiness, thankful that my mother, and my rooster, could be safe in eternal Paradise.

Diane was comforting John as he cried for the rooster's long dead corpse, and we all took them back inside for a while, just so they could feel a bit better.

John buried his friend out back, in a grave next to the living chickens.

I smiled throughout this whole funerary ceremony, saying a few words for my little guy, my rooster, saying he was in a better place, and that I knew so.

I also said, "We all have a chance at this better place, even just in life for now. The undead do, eidolons do, whores do, the insane do. And I do. We all can live in Paradise, together, and not alone."

Abbot said, "Holy shit. Like fucking Jesus would say. Quick, you gotta bless the grave."

I smiled, and said, "Bejesus in Heaven, hallelujah almighty, I bless this grave in peace."

John wiped off his tears, and said, "Thank you, Jesus girl. Thank you."

I placed my black tulip on the grave, as the others placed flowers on the grave.

The Madame came out back, and said, "Fucking hell, what on Earth is going on?? Are you all insane or something? Quit crying for a chicken, and get back to work before I burn your minds into nothing, if there's anything left that is!"

We said goodbye to Diane and John, and they drove off down the road as a couple, and I got back to cleaning the house.

42

I watched, as Abbot cast another illusion of bestiality… this time with a leopard.

There were a lot of viewers tonight. We assured them it was all safe…

Which still didn't stop Abbot, after the act was done, to command the leopard to prowl amongst the audience, scaring the bejesus out of absolutely every filthy degenerate in the room.

They ran screaming from Abbot and her illusion, as Abbot commanded the leopard to kill, her cackling in glee.

I walked up to her, in the now empty theater, as her fake leopard stroked against her naked legs and she pet its chin, wiping the tears of laughter off her face.

"WOOHOO!! What a fucking rush. I *always* wanted to do that! *Always!!* HAHAHA!! I turn in my resignation, tonight, and the MADAME can suck the dick instead of me!!" Abbot said, then roared in triumph.

"That's your choice, Abbot. I respect it. A lot. That took a shit ton of guts." I said.

She sighed out, after laughing for so long, and said, "I think I've learned enough here, anyway. The Madame's end goal wasn't to keep us as her whores forever, but to eventually have us liberate ourselves from the shackles of the society we live in ourselves. I guess."

"That's a very good way to put it." I said, "What are you going to do now?"

"Beats me. I'm gonna probably bum around America for a while, I think. Just go camping! I always wanted to see Niagara Falls. I know it will probably be disappointing, compared to the wonder I can cast with my little ring, but I always wanted to see that roaring water." Abbot said, putting on her clothes again. She waved a hand at the leopard, the leopard bowed to her, and disappeared.

"...Can Luke and I join you?" I asked.

"Fuck! Let's bring 'em all! All you guys are seriously my best friends, in this shitty life. I finally hooked my parents up, they're married and happy, and I can ditch them and never have to look at their ugly faces ever again!

"I want Tas. All the time, everywhere with me. I don't care that she's a woman, she's fucking better than anything I've ever done for these bastards. Seriously! I can't even get off with a customer anymore! I give fake orgasms every night, but eventually I just gave up on moaning all together! I'm sick of that particular, very boring, mundane illusion.

"And Francesca is like, she's my best gal. Her and I were the rival bitches at the start, but we eventually allied together since we're so powerful!! No one could stop us, me and Francesca, and we will take over this entire world with our combined strength!! WE ARE THE MASTERS OF THIS BROTHEL!!

"I miss Diane, but I think she's got the best thing going for her. She wrapped up all of our failure, and even gave it some love that we never could. Those two are going to be the happiest, and they sent me pictures of their trip so far. They look... They look at peace.

"Malena, ooooh Malena... You poor, confused, lovely, loving heart. She's already improved Dragon Guy to a new extreme!! Did I tell you who's going to be our next prime minister?" Abbot said.

"No way. Dragon Guy??" I said.

"You bet. Malena gave him what he always wanted, and now he's got courage, strength, and is satisfied, for once. I want Malena with us, even though they were thinking of getting hitched. As something poety she might say, 'Huge hearts doth not belong to one man!' Her heart belongs to us, her friends.

"And you. I know you want to be some apocalyptic harbinger, or something like that, but I want you to rethink that. Life's not so bad, and I think you know this. You're probably my best friend, in truth, even though I hate your guts sometimes." Abbot said.

"And I you, Abbot. But it's a loving hate." I said.

"Got that right! Let's go, and tell the Madame off together! I can't wait for my new life!!" Abbot said, took my arm, and we strolled to the Madame.

The Madame smiled to us, in her office, after we said we were quitting and going to the U.S.

She simply said, "You belong to me, girls."

Abbot said, "...No, are you deaf or something in your weird old age? I quit."

"I'm sorry, Abbot, but by the contract you signed, you cannot quit." the Madame said.

"...But I didn't even sign my real name! My name is 'Abbot' and not... What did I sign, anyway? Must've forgot." Abbot said.

"That name belongs to me, Abbot. Your first name. You can keep the last name, Abbot, even be called by it... but your real name is... mine." the Madame said.

I said, "...What contract?"

"Oh, you didn't sign one, since you're my protege, Mary. We even have the same first name... I think of you as my daughter, at times, and I know that you will be a great harbinger of the apocalypse. I think we'll just state the obvious, and call you Jesus Jane... Sounds catchy, huh?" the Madame said.

"B-But I don't want to start the apocalypse." I said.

"And I don't want to be a whore!" Abbot said.

"You will change your minds. Perhaps you two need to switch jobs for a while? You can work on your back, Mary, and you can clean up her messes, Abbot, until you finally have found your proper places… Haha…" the Madame said, "Now, if you're done complaining, I expect you both to be happy, happy, happy! That's what draws in the crowd."

And before we knew what we were doing, we both said, "Yes, Madame."

We then walked out of the office, disoriented, disillusioned… and in despair.

43

I cried on Luke's shoulder, as I was in this skimpy outfit, the curtain on the window closed so that people would think I was working... which I technically was, because Luke had paid again to waste my time. But the timer had just again buzzed, signalling his time was up.

"Y-You don't h-have enough for a whore even all night. I c-can't let y-you do this... I can just put on an act... Please, it's not like it would be new for me, fucking a stranger to get something out of them..." I said, moping against him.

"Can you just act really bad at your job?? That'd help, right??" Luke said.

"It won't help a thing, because... I have to work, if I want to get Abbot and the others out of their contracts. That's her one foothold on me, those stupid contracts on my friends..." I said, "It was all an illusion, this whole magic thing... I should've known from the start."

Abbot was shaking in the corner, dressed in the maid outfit, sweeping, and sweeping, and sweeping, even though it was spotless. She muttered to herself, "Joanne? Lily? What is my name..."

Luke looked at her, back at me, and said, "Is there anyone that can help?? I don't like this, and I'll talk with the Madame right this instant-"

"Please don't. You wouldn't be the first person she's destroyed who messes in her work." I said.

"But- What does she want of you?? Destroy the world?? That's crazy!!" Luke said.

"It is." I said, "All I know is that she is immortal, very powerful, and hates everything about this life. I saw it in her eyes, and I think someone stole her death."

Someone knocked on the door, and in force of habit, Abbot opened it. She said to the man and his friends, "Shit. Can't you see we're busy??"

"...Isn't this what you're supposed to do? C'mon! It's our buddy's birthday!" a tourist said, and then they cheered for each other.

Abbot slammed the door in their faces.

I sighed, got up, walked to the door, opened it, and said, "Bring the whole lot! I'm taking all comers! C'mon in, boys!"

Luke tried to drag me away from the door, as the tourists cheered for me and approached, but someone beat them to the front of the line.

The hooded woman said, "I'll take you for the rest of the night. Sorry, dudes, but this beautiful person is mine."

The men all started arguing, but the woman put down her hood, smiled at them, and they gasped.

One said, "...Like a fucking angel. Ok, let's... Let's let the ladies have their fun! Hell yeah! You get her, girl!" and then they cheered for this beautiful, angelic woman.

Abbot said to her, "Oh... Hello, Saint. Long time no see. Come in."

Saint, the prostitute Abbot told me about who had Jesus in her bed, walked in, as Abbot closed behind her.

I sighed, and said, "Look, I've got to meet a quota-"

Saint paid an astounding amount to me, all in cash, as I gasped, and she said, "Here. This will satisfy your overlord for now. It was very difficult to work up this amount, so let us use our time thriftily."

I said, "...You took the dicks, so I wouldn't have to. You really are a saint."

"That's what they call me, and that is my only name now. I actually never recovered my past name from the Madame, but I realized I never even needed it." Saint said, as Luke and I sat on the bed, and she sat on the chair.

Abbot continued to sweep.

Saint said, "I believe you can free the others, but you must have faith. Things will be difficult, they will be hellish, but you do not have to go down this road made out for you."

"How? I don't know what to do. I've tried incantations, all sorts of spells, even tried attacking the Madame when I thought she was vulnerable. She is an impenetrable force of the mind, her dreams are complete darkness, and if I try to use fire, she puts it out and laughs at me, saying that she doesn't like smoke." I said, "I smoke a lot of cigarettes now, in the rooms, just to annoy her."

Saint smiled, and said, "It is good you are being so defiant. Magic… was always just a trick. It does not belong to God, Satan, or any other, it has always served itself, as old as the world. Some become very attuned to this power, but in the end, it will still only serve itself. Your dilemma is trapped in this magic, spiralling out of control, so I urge you to rely on mundanity instead of powers inconceivable. It may save your soul."

"But that's all I have! I have nothing else strong enough to beat the Madame! All of us use magic in defense, in our jobs, and just to live! If I give it up, I'll have nothing else left. I need to give up my decency, serve the Madame, and if she is merciful, she will release the others." I said.

"That sounds like what she wants you to think. Did she inject this idea into your head?" Saint said.

"…No, I don't think so… I just feel like that is the logical conclusion…" I said.

"Even she doesn't need magic, and her true power stemmed from mundane psychology. The magic is just the icing on the cake, and fear is her weapon." Saint said, "You need to give up her weapon, your weapon, and your fear, or you will be lost."

I looked at Chuck on my waist, and said, "This is my only weapon... a silly princess wand..."

"And it is seeped in magic. Perhaps... a talisman only has power if you put your power in it. I have never seen the Madame wield something so ridiculous. Why is that?" Saint said.

"...That's true... She doesn't have any little trinket or anything..." I said.

"And I never needed one either, and I am the most successful prostitute in the world. I once believed in fairies and princesses... and they gave me a sort of strength, as I wielded my magic princess wand after my family died in a fire... but in the end I realized that was childish, silly, and ultimately a waste of wonder, seeing so much beauty in natural life itself." Saint said.

I said, "...You wielded Chuck before me?"

"Is that its name now? I always thought the wand was given to me by my fairy godfather... It was a birthday present from my real father, before he died, and it helped keep his memory alive, with this wand. That was the only power it ever had for me, in truth, a memory. I threw the wand out, because I needed to take on a more mature pose in my profession, and it was very difficult for me. But I believe my father is still with me, and I never needed a material possession to keep his memory alive." Saint said.

I looked down at Chuck, and turned it into a sword. I turned myself into a demon.

I said, "If I destroy the world, I'll destroy the Madame first."

Saint immediately... hugged me.

I didn't know what to do, but she said, "You poor soul... I am sorry that you ever believed this form was really you. You were never a demon, a Devil's Daughter, or belonged in Hell... You are blessed, always, even through the pain. I love you. Can you remember what your name is?"

I looked at her, blinked, and said, "Mary Jane. I was named Mary for my mother... Mary. Jane is just a middle name, and I hated the name Mary for as long as I lived, as I hated my mother. I don't anymore, and am proud to be named after her. I prefer going by the name Jane, over Mary, or even Mary Jane."

"You have been named for your family, by your family, who love you. Your family who loves you may not always be blood related, but the ones who love you will always be your family. I am glad that you can remember your name." Saint said.

Abbot looked at her, and said, "...Can you help me find mine?"

Saint sighed, and said, "Alas, I feel magic is coursing through you, the Madame's magic, as it coursed through me. Your name hasn't been stolen by a contract, by a piece of paper... you gave it up. I gave up mine willingly as well. But as all my old family is dead, I have decided to become Saint, and let all be my family. This approach may not work as well for you as it has for me. Resist the allure of complete oblivion, and try to remember who you are. It will come at its own pace, if you seek.

"Seek and yeh shall find. The truth can be found in evidence, fact, and your own will. Seek the truth, hunger for it, and do not fall into the lies of others. This is true clarity, and there is nothing magical about it." Saint said, "Now, I believe you should all stay somewhere safe for a while, hide from magic, ignore it, do not look for symbols and signs that will cause you evil. Go home, and I will take your place for tonight."

Saint took off her hooded robe, and we gasped at her beauty.

She practically shone with the light, her features were the best in the world.

I put on my rag shirt, my first shirt, and pants, and Saint opened the door for us to leave, and the three of us shifted into the night, allowing

Saint's first customer to walk in beside us, who she greeted with the most kind smile ever and a wave.

I realized I had forgotten Chuck, in the bed of the little girl who held it in the past, whose parents died in a fire, now a Saint.

44

Abbot said, as we were in Francesca's once sex pad, "...So my talisman, my ring, is actually evil? How can that be? It is a clerical object blessed by God."

"Mine's just an indeterminate piece of goldish looking metal, to me." I said, showing off my own ring, "The only reason I keep it is because it is a gift from Luke."

Luke rubbed the back of his head, looking nervous, and said, "It's actually a big regret of mine, stealing it from that minister... I'd give it back if I could, but I already gave it to you."

"And I like it, so it's mine now. Priests don't need stupid rings anyway. I mean, you saw Saint, right? She looked holier than any priest I've *ever* seen, and she was completely naked." I said.

"Holier than my dad, anyway." Abbot said, "My dad had relations with a laywoman, and could've been excommunicated if he did not step down peacefully. He lied about it, kept it hidden, as my mother did to keep him safe. His whole job caused him sin, after sin, even if he was a holy man."

Luke said, "Huh. If he never took that job, it wouldn't have been a sin, right?"

"I suppose so... Really the ecclesiastical rings are *also* passed on to the next priest, and not to the priest's daughter who came about from a forbidden relationship..." Abbot said, looking at the ring, "I was just so proud of him, every single Sunday. I'd sit in the pew, praying with my mother, and think, that's my father. That man, giving a heartwarming sermon, consecrating the host, and even blessing us as we left to come back next week. I thought of the church more as my dad's house, rather than the Lord's."

I said, "Can you remember what he called you? What your mother called you?"

"...I don't know... I call myself Abbot, because that's my dad's last name... I had a different last name, I think, because there is no way my dad wouldn't have been found out if Someone Abbot was running around when I was little, with the same last name." Abbot said.

I said, "Your parents are married now, right? So the last name is actually correct?"

"Well, yes, in a sense. It's not the name I grew up with, but it can definitely be my name now if I choose it." Abbot said, "I just... would really like to know my first name... It's weird, but I haven't thought how strange it is being a girl called Abbot, a last name, in a long time. I was proud of it, at the start, but I wonder what I gave up..."

Luke said, "Can't we just ask your parents?"

Abbot said, "...It's worth a shot. Let's go to them, as soon as possible. This is very frustrating to me. Oh, I'll just seek them out and read them-"

"No." I said, "Let's just do this... like a normal, mundane person. Let's go."

We went to the bus station, waiting like hobos, travelers, random passersby. We got on as people were trying to sleep in the bus, in uncomfortable positions. Like a normal bus, everyone was silent, and we sat nervously, hoping none would try to steal our stuff, attack us or anything. Luke was the most comfortable, being used to this sort of lifestyle before. He said, "It's no fun sleeping on a bus. You wake up without getting any rest, angry, disgruntled... It's a pain. I actually got in a fight with my brother after we took the night bus, we were so tired and uncomfortable, the first time I went to Europe."

"What happened then?" I asked.

"We split up, but when we both decided independently we had enough of Barcelona... we met at the bus station by chance, and got back together again. I guess our paths diverged and converged, all thanks to the bus." Luke said.

We got off the bus, in a secluded area at the edge of the city, and Luke said, "Oh, I'm getting a call from Tas. Actually... she also sent me a shit ton of texts, asking where you were, Abbot."

Abbot said, "You have my girlfriend's work phone number?"

Luke said, "Just in case. I guess she's really worried about you. Do you want to-"

Abbot grabbed the phone out of Luke's hand and answered, saying, "TAS! I'm so frightened, and scared, and really miss you."

Tas said, "...What's wrong, Abbot? You don't have to be scared. The Madame said you were missing, and I've been so worried-"

"Don't trust her!! She's trying to steal our names, our souls, and is probably the Devil!!" Abbot said.

"...I think you need a good rest, Abbot. I know, she has magic, but good magic. She helps people with it, gives them jobs, positions, a place in society. Please come home?" Tas said.

"Nonono, just trust me, Tas. I *can't even remember my name.* D-Do you still have yours? Can you tell me what your last name is, Tashan?" Abbot said.

"...I took the name Tas because it's- It's more feminine. Tashan is a boy's name. My last name was always different, every time my dad and I took a job... Just- Please tell me where you are?" Tas said.

"Please!! Tell me your last name, and I'll trust you." Abbot said.

"...Jacobs. It's Jacobs, because my father is an American, like I am if you believe I inherited my nationality from my father..." Tas said.

"Tashan Jacobs. Thank you, Tas. That means a lot to me, and I'll always love you for being you." Abbot said, and then hung up.

I said, "Why did you do that?? She could've helped us!"

Abbot shook her head, and said, "She could be one of them now. We can't trust anyone. Also, *American??* Are all my friends from the pig eating corn country??"

"Hey, you eat a lot of pigs too." I said.

"But *still...* you eat bacon on everything, bacon ice cream, bacon at every gas station and in the vending machines." Abbot said.

Luke said, "Bacon vending machines? Not a bad idea, actually."

Abbot sighed, and showed us to her parents' house.

"...So I see you found some American friends." Abbot's dad said to her, after he invited us inside.

"Well, you know they're not all bad. They're attractive, loose with their money, that sort of thing." Abbot said.

Her mom immediately hugged her, and said, "Ik ben zo blij dat je thuis bent gekomen."

"Alleen voor een bezoek, moeder. Dan ga ik... weer aan het werk. Ja. Ik wil u vragen, vooral u... Wat is mijn naam?" Abbot said.

Her mother blinked, and her father said, "We have company, Tinneke. Please, let them in on the conversation..."

Her mother said, "I do not understand your question, dochter."

I said, "...Is dochter her name?"

Luke said, "...That just means daughter."

"Oh. Duh." I said.

Abbot looked at us, back at her parents, and said, "I think... I have deja vu, or amnesia, or something. Both. Deja amnesia, and I have a hard time remembering some things now..."

Her father clenched his fists, and said, "...I knew I should've never allowed you to take up such a job, but it was not my choice for you at the time. Who hit you?? Just because I was a priest doesn't mean I don't know how to throw a punch."

Abbot said, "...No one, Pa. Just... please. Call me by my real name."

Her dad sighed, and said, "You even talk like these Americans now. I am sorry... daughter... I was never there for you when you grew up, besides briefly, and did not know how much you could change. I want to accept you as an Abbot, as your mother has accepted the name, and bring you fully under my wing. Is that a right euphemism?"

Her mother said, "Ik ben nu echt zo ontzettend blij. We konden elkaar zelfs nooit in het openbaar aanraken, maar nu is dat voorbij en zijn we vrij."

Abbot said, "But- But- I want to accept this name, I really do, I just am worried what I am giving up."

Her mother said, "You are giving up nothing, daughter. You have always been an Abbot. It was so very difficult having no father for you, as you know, but your father did all he could, even working side jobs just for you. Remember how he got you that puppy? You were the happiest little girl in the world."

Abbot said, "...Yes. I remember... And I accept the name... Abbot... It is the right decision. I want to give this back, Pa, because I don't feel good about you stealing from the ministry like that, just to get your daughter some jewelry..."

Abbot handed her father her ring, and her father sighed, taking it back. He said, "It will be difficult to tell them how this *also* went missing, just like my ethics, but I believe I can get them to understand. The Catholic Church is a very forgiving entity."

Abbot said, "Thank you, Pa. I am so proud of you, and you make my day whenever I see you, because I could never see you before."

Abbot and her dad hugged, and her mother invited us to watch football, you know, soccer for Americans, with them.

"Oh, Anke, please get some snacks from the cupboard, if you could." her mother said.

Abbot didn't even respond at first, but then did a double take at her mother, and smiled and laughed in glee.

"Anke!! My name is Anke!! I'm so happy!! I remember it now!! You always called me Klein Anke!! I love you, mother, and you, father, and even you two, you hippie Americans, Mary and Luke. I'm so happy!!" Anke said, and grabbed some chips, and hugged each and all of us.

45

Anke's parents let us stay the night, and in the morning Anke gave me a sweatshirt as it was getting kind of chilly out. I thanked her, put it on over my rag shirt, and said I really didn't want to have to use magic to change my body temperature.

We sat on the bench outside, looking at the morning dew and rising sun. Anke said, "It was always so easy, to get whatever I wanted, with magic. Change the temperature, teleport myself a snack, even read some minds to pass the time. I feel a little disoriented without it."

"I think it's the safer option. Do you feel free now?" I asked.

"Yes, strangely, since I guess I always did have my name. Anke Abbot. But what was weird, was that I was tempted to use magic and-" Anke said.

"What? No! Why did you do that, Anke??" I said.

"Don't worry. I couldn't cast an imaginary spark. I put all my magic out through the talisman, and now I've got no conduit at all. I don't know how to do what you can, wave your hands and make fire." Anke said, "I guess I've always been sort of jealous of you for that."

I shrugged, and said, "A person I am related to was once an actual angel, now a horrid demon, the Devil. I had a grasp on all sorts of this stuff before I came here. Like a succubus, I could vanish into your dreams, like a hellbeast, I can command the fires of Hell itself. I now know how to change myself at will, from demon or not. I even used to know how to cast an illusion, unintentionally, and walk around naked whenever I pleased."

"You just have magic all around you. I can see why the Madame thinks you're powerful." Anke said.

"I don't want any of this power, especially not the Madame's power. I didn't *try* to be naked, I just had no shame, and the illusion reflected that. The dream thing is kinda fun, but it can be scary too, because you never know what a dream will throw at you. It can be a nightmare at the whiff of a feeling. As soon as I saw that I could look like me, like how I always wanted to, the body changed into who I was, a human. I admit the fire thing is kind of useful, but really only just to start a cigarette or if we're camping." I said.

"Gosh… I just want to go camping now… It gets more and more appealing every time I think about it… But… camping alone sounds very lame. I want our buddies, and everyone the Madame has ensnared, to be able to go camping too." Anke said.

"It's got a lot of good places in the U.S., and we make a lot of money on tourist camping, even from just within the U.S. itself. We can go to YellowStone, Niagara Falls, Badlands, all sorts of other little places littering the entire country… We can make s'mores, go swimming every day, sit up at night and just tell stories by the fire while we get drunk… It'll be a great adventure." I said.

Luke came out for a smoke, as Anke sighed and said, "Sounds too good to be true. But thank you for giving me hope. What is our next plan of attack? Just get a gun and shoot her down? That sounds pretty normal and non magical."

"Hmm… I guess that would work. I'm thinking a good shotgun, just so we know we got her." I said.

Luke nearly dropped his pipe he was smoking, and said, "Um. I think you shouldn't try to kill your past boss. That usually doesn't end well for most people, everyone involved."

I said, "But she's like a super evil bitch boss."

"Isn't everyone's last boss?" Luke said.

"I guess so… and I guess it might not work, either, with her being somehow still alive. Probably just get up and laugh at us, like she's good at doing." I said. I felt the anger at such a figure, such a creature that could mock us indefinitely, take hold over us and force us to do *unnameable acts for her own twisted schemes…*

I felt so angry, fuming on the bench. Abbot stared at me hard for some reason, and Luke…

Luke sat before me and… began to draw on a pocket notebook.

"What are you doing? Do you think this is really a good time to draw me naked?" I said.

"I just want you to see yourself how we are seeing you right now. It may be pretty, it may be not, but I think it is perfectly acceptable."

"I don't know what you mean, but- Oh. I see…" I said.

Luke showed me the picture he was working on, and it was a demon me. I didn't even realize I was doing that.

"Well. At least let me pose. I like doing that." I said, and got off the bench, posing for Luke.

"That's a pose? You're not even doing anything." *Anke said.*

"A good pose doesn't have to be an action pose or anything. Just showing the feeling you want to portray." I said.

"Exactly. You are very blunt sometimes, but that makes it easier for you to be blunt with your feelings as well, open, if you'd like a better word than blunt." *Luke said.*

"Nah. Blunt is fine. I want what I want, I take what I take, and I show what I show." I said.

Luke showed me the picture.

I said, "Oh! I'm smiling."

Luke said, "Yes. You are."

I continued smiling, and hugged him.

Anke said, "...You two have a really weird relationship. But it's kind of sweet. Well, let's get out of my parents' hair, after breakfast. I want to hunt down the Madame and save my friends."

We went back inside, and Anke's dad looked at me in demon form, and shouted, "By *Jesus Christ!! Begone, demon, and leave this holy house-* Er. I'm sorry. I thought I saw something, for a second there... I think this whole shift in my life has been very stressful."

I had quickly turned back into a human, and Anke's mom said, "Rest, my husband. I will work on the food. Anke, could you please set the table?"

"Right away, mother." Anke said, and set the table.

We sat and ate pancakes with bacon in them, with strawberries with sugar. I teased Anke about her delicious pig pancakes, and Anke blushed.

We left the Abbots after a great, but quick, breakfast, and went off into the day to conquer our nightmare, our past teacher and boss.

46

We hazarded to pick up some things from Francesca's once sex pad, and when we got in, we found her lounging on the couch, staring at us with a cold look.

"But I- You gave me the key to this place." I said.

"I never needed keys. I thought just giving up the symbol would be enough for me... and I like what you did with this place, Luke, Mary... but I think I want it back now. I'm going to make love here, and I need somewhere secluded... I think you should go back home, Mary, Abbot... It would be best for you both, the whole job dodging thing notwithstanding..." Francesca said, getting up from the couch to face us.

We could practically feel the magic in the air, as Francesca gripped a pencil in her hand.

"What will it be? Will you fight me for such a petty, insignificant amount of territory? Or will you step in line and get back to work?" Francesa said.

Anke said, "Francesca... You know you don't need to do this. I know you must've signed a contract too-"

Francesca said, "I did. And it is my power. You don't get anything for free. The Madame is my business partner, my backer, without her my entire corporation would fall to nothing."

I said, "Corporation?"

"I own many, even though my name doesn't officially stand on the rosters. I pull the puppets' strings, and they dance. Would you like me to demonstrate?" Francesca said, and swished her pencil violently at Anke.

Anke twisted forward, and... began dancing to music that wasn't there.

"How about you, maid? I think Abbot needs a partner." Francesca said, swished her pencil, and made me dance hand in hand with Anke. "And I think I'll let you draw this, this heartwarming scene, artist. *Draw.*" Francesca said, swished her pencil at Luke... and Luke didn't do anything.

Luke said, "Why? I don't find anything inspiring, amusing, or heartwarming in this scene. I just see a bully. I really don't like bullies."

Francesca faltered, and then said, *"Draw, damnit!! BY THE MADAME!!"* and swished her pencil over and over at Luke, like she was trying to cut him to pieces, but Luke simply watched her sadly.

"You expect to force me to do something with just a pencil? It doesn't even look that sharp." Luke said.

I did notice the pencil was rather dull, and Anke and I slowed our dancing pace.

Luke continued, "I don't find any power in just a pencil, or even the Madame. You're both just bullies, and for a bully you don't give them power over you. At best, you ignore them, at worst you push them away and get back to your day. I won't give into a bully, Francesca, dull pencil or no. I also prefer drawing in pen."

Francesca said, "I'll... I'll use my business, and destroy you. I'll find out what makes you tick, yeah, and I'll make sure you don't have it. I'll make sure whoever you work for fires you on the spot-"

"I'm independent, Francesca, an independent artist and writer." Luke said.

Francesca slumped her shoulders, and we stopped dancing.

Francesca said, "...That was always my dream. To work for myself, even be an artist on my own... That... How did you know that?"

Luke said, "It was nothing about you. It was my choice, and it is my life. Not everything revolves around you."

Francesca snapped the pencil in her hand in fury, and said, "You. All of you. You think you can escape and live on your own? The world revolves around the sun, and we revolve around the stronger force. We need others' strength, if we want to survive. I am Francesca, and I accept this."

Anke went to Francesca, and slapped her hard.

Francesca took the slap, and didn't turn her head back at Anke.

"That's for being such an idiot. You're so smart, yet so fucking stupid. You need me, dummy. Without me, you wouldn't have half the work in the house you get done. You work on *my* profits, not yours. Without me, you probably wouldn't even have a single friend. Without me... You are only Francesca. I want to give you your name back, Mary does too, as she helped give me mine back, and Luke does as well, even just being a normal person, who doesn't understand us or our powers." Anke said.

Francesca looked at Anke, and said, "B-But the fine print. I read it, I understood it, even if it was in horribly legal language, magical language, and it said if I want my name back, everything I've done for the Madame will cease to be mine."

I said, "I don't think it was ever yours, if it was never under a name you chose. It always belonged only to someone named Francesca, who belonged to the Madame. It's kind of like a scheme in Hell, where the end lord is always Satan, no matter the hellish archdukes and hellish viscounts."

"B-But everything I've done, I am so proud of being able to do it. Certainly my action speaks for my ownership?" Francesca said.

I said, "I thought you understood business. The only power is money, Francesca. Your sacrifices and diligence means nothing, unless you get money. We work because we want to fuel the rest of our life, not to fuel work."

Francesca looked at her feet, and said, "I guess I… just created another monster, and fell in love with it again too… I- I- relinquish my services from you, Madame."

We could hear the Madame laugh on the wind from the open window, and Francesca dropped her broken pencil to the floor.

Francesca was crying, and said, "And now, all I ever loved is gone. I have absolutely nothing."

I said, "What about that lover you said you wanted to bring over?"

She just hugged me.

"That was going to be your artist. I would've forced him into being mine, like the monster I am, but… I suppose I have no claim on him, especially not in love." Francesca said.

Luke sighed, and sat with Anke on the couch, as I hugged Francesca.

I said, "Aww. That's so sweet. Luke, don't you feel special for the intent to fuck?"

"It is kind of flattering… but I don't think it would've happened like you imagine, Francesca." Luke said.

"It obviously didn't, as I was waiting just for you." Francesca said to Luke, and sighed in my arms. "I am Francesca Smith, and I am sorry."

"Apology accepted, Miss Smith." Luke said.

Francesca said, "I just thought, y'know, we really got along as I was a third wheel to you guys on our date… I thought, y'know, maybe I was actually the date, sometimes, fantasized about it even… and then you move in *here*… What can I say. Old habits die hard."

I smiled to Francesca, and said, "I'm sure the second girlfriend fantasy is always what Luke wanted-"

"No, no, no… Sorry, Jane." Luke said, "But even though that *sounds* nice, in practice I've seen it doesn't really work. Do you dream of that?"

I shrugged, and said, "I always thought it would be neat to be a mistress."

Luke laughed, and said, "If you are, then you're probably also my wife."

I smiled at him, and said, "And that's the answer I was hoping for. Let's go out and get… weird, European burgers, that definitely aren't burgers with all the weird stuff they put on them, but they'll do."

We left the pad, grabbing some supplies, stuffing them in backpacks, and went out for lunch.

47

"I will never draw again." Francesca said, chomping on a burger.

Luke said, "I think you will. The time I wrote for real I had a psychotic break, the very first time I heard voices, and I thought I'd never write again. Now I write books, as well as the art. You'll be able to draw again."

I said, "I think your power wasn't in the pencil, Francesca, it was in the Madame."

Francesca said, "I think you're both right. This is just a bad experience... and even if I won't be able to make my drawings move, I can figure out some normal way to fill that hole in my soul that was filled by magic."

Anke said, "That guy. Over there, the one staring at you. Let him fill that hole."

"...Why him? Is he someone important here?" Francesca said.

"No, but he likes you, obviously. Don't think about it so hard, man." Anke said.

Francesca shrugged, and went to talk to the guy, who was very nervous around Francesca, especially since she made the first move to come up to him.

204

They were soon flirting and laughing, and Francesca came back with a number on a napkin. The guy paid for his food, was going to leave, but bowed to Francesca before he left, smiled, waved, and left the restaurant.

"What's with the bow?" I asked.

"I have no clue. I thought I could figure him out just by reading his mind, but it was silent. Maybe he's dumb?" Francesca said.

Anke burst out laughing, and said, "Now you know what we're going through. The magic is gone... and the real magic can begin. You looked like you definitely had the hots for him."

Francesca said, "He was so... different! I couldn't place why, but I had no power over him, besides just my looks and intellect. It was a very strange feeling."

Luke said, "Hey, that's a lot of power already, looks and intellect... I think you'll like living in the mundane world again."

We left, and stayed away from the house. We didn't want to be caught in the Madame's spider webs unprepared. We cafe hopped, bar hopped, and eventually were at a unique squat in Holland, a legal squat, dancing with the other hobos, squatters, and party people.

Francesca danced with her bowing guy. She flirted nicely with him, calling him her royal guard, and they got off very well.

So well, Francesca even decided to take him into a back room to make love.

We all applauded, us party goers, after the final moan was uttered after some very loud lovemaking.

Francesca came out of the back room, smiling in content... and then Malena followed.

Francesca did a double take at Malena, stuttered, as Anke, Luke, and I were in shock and the others were all cheering even louder.

Malena kissed Francesca on the cheek, and said, "That's what you were missing, Francesca. I hope you enjoyed my show. I want to warn you all that the Madame will find you eventually, just as easily I did, but she won't cause you so much pleasure. I will meet you under the biggest bridge in the city."

Francesca said, "B-But I could've sworn you were a man. I could've sworn you were someone else. How can we trust you??"

Malena giggled, bowed, and walked off into the crowd, dancing with the others… when we tried to catch her, she had disappeared as another individual, and we had no clue where she went.

We carefully got underneath the bridge, and found Malena cutting herself in silence.

I gasped, and ran up to her, as she opened her body and let it heal after every cut.

I said, "Don't do that, Malena. It will be ok."

Malena said, "I just find it pleasurable. Really. I like being able to heal my body after every slash, every wound. It shows I am strong."

I said, "…Ok. Why are you here, then?"

Malena frowned at me, and said, "Please cut the binds out of me."

I said, "I can understand, really, and all we need to do is break her binds, and her contract will be powerless-"

"But I did not sign a contract. I gave my body to the Madame, completely, fully, everything, all of it. This body is hers, and through it she sees you. I am very sorry… I do not feel pain in my body, pleasure, anything… I've changed it so many times, every which way… I just know I am Malena, for you people, anyway." Malena said, and continued slicing her arm, letting the wounds heal.

The Madame said through Malena's mouth, "This is the power of magic, Mary Jane. It is not some silly force that can be wished away. It is truth, power, and life. You can defeat me… If you defeat all of these entities. You must destroy magic, and with it the world. It is what is keeping me alive, powerlessly powerful, just like-"

Malena said, "Just like me. It was a cruel joke, magic. We both thought with one more lay in magic's embrace, we could maybe feel something again. I feel the Madame, always. I was always-"

The Madame said, "Always with you, as I was with Malena, with Francesca, with Abbot. You are a part of me as well, and we are all together, every lifeform. We must-"

Malena said, "Please just cut it out of me."

Malena gave me the knife, as I stuttered, and the Madame was silent.

Malena, or the Madame, said, "We take a little bit of every soul, as we take their body. We take a little bit of others, with just their words, their touch. Cut it out of me, and let me be free."

Malena then knelt before me.

They said, "The heart is my bind to my body. Cut it out of me, and let that be my end."

I did not want to kill Malena.

Malena changed her form into that of the Madame, and I wanted to kill that.

I threw the knife in the river.

Malena sighed, and changed... back into a scrawny, crippled woman.

48

Luke carried Malena through the streets to the hospital. Malena said, "Please... I don't want to go to another hospital... Just... please... Leave me."

Luke said to her, "No, Malena. We at least need to get you a wheelchair. It hurts me seeing you like this."

Malena said, "I... I feel the pain now. And I am so happy for it. I just don't want you all- All to feel my pain like this..."

I held Malena's hand, and said, "You've got the biggest heart amongst us, Malena. We all love you."

Malena said, "That knife... That knife was... was my only possession from my home. It was my one piece of Honduras. It was one of my family's... someone who cared for me that I cannot remember, and gave it to me, not as a cruel joke because I could never use it, but because he loved me, and wanted me to remember him. I am... I am sad that I cannot anymore.

"I came here for aid, mostly so my family could get rid of me and not feel guilty, and then the Madame found me, after all methods of medicine were ineffective.

"She cured me, with what I never had before. She cured me with her very own body. It was... It was marvellous. It was something I could never, ever have. I felt complete. And then the Madame gave me more.

"Now I do not even have my own body, or anything. I will never be able to work, like this, and I will always be a burden on others." Malena said.

I said, "That's not true, Malena. You were never a burden. You make everyone feel happy, all the time, even without having sex with them."

"They were only being too nice to me." Malena said.

We got to the hospital, and I stayed beside Malena in her bed, as the others got a hostel room.

I looked sadly on her broken body, so gentle and caring, and so fragile, as she slept.

I woke up in the morning, with her laying in the bed and looking at me.

"I really did love every single person who I could. I wanted to show them that they can have love as I have received. It wasn't just work for me, it was a way of life." Malena said.

"I think that's very beautiful, Malena. What brought this topic on?" I said.

"You just seem like you want to be a savior, as I wanted to be a lover. Can you save this?" Malena said, and waved a hand gently at her body.

"I don't think I can, Malena. But your mind, your heart, and your soul are strong. You can find other callings, I know. I just want you to know… I love you too. May I hug you? Please. Very gently." I said.

Malena looked at me sadly, and opened her arms slowly, difficultly, for a hug.

We sat for a long time, just hugging each other.

Malena said, "It's weird my last time was with Francesca. She told me she was a virgin, before we did it, and based on her body language… I kinda believe her."

I laughed, and said, "I don't think it will be your last time. I hope."

Malena sighed, and said, "You are very optimistic. I like that, and it makes me happy. Happy people always are easier to please."

"So you really know your name and everything?" I asked.

"I know I call myself Malena, and that is who I choose to be. I don't care what anyone else calls me, I am Malena, and that is who I am." Malena said.

"What if- What if we got a really gentle, really nice prostitute to lay with you? And one of us can chaperone, just in case-" I said.

"I don't want that, Mary. I want what I had, to make love freely, and not pitied or cared for. That's why I said it was my last time, because that was the last time I felt that feeling, like with the Madame." Malena said.

"...Ok... I guess, if you feel that way. That makes sense, really. No one likes being pitied if they can help it." I said.

"Will you be another of my caretakers now, too? I wouldn't mind, since you're my friend." Malena said.

"Well... Yes. I will, if that's what you want. I would find it very enjoyable to care for a friend like you." I said.

"Good. Now know that you don't have to. I just... will live like I have, getting aid, and hopefully I can find some sort of happiness again." Malena said.

I said, "We were thinking of going camping, before we all realized we were trapped by the Madame and magic. Would you care to join us?"

Malena opened her eyes in surprise, and said, "Are you sure?"

"I am positive, my friend." I said.

"Then- Then- Yes. Just for a while, because I won't be able to take all that travelling with my body. Maybe we can just go to the Black Forest, if we could? Just for a bit? I love nature." Malena said.

"I think that would be amazing, Malena. We can travel with you for as long as you like." I said.

Malena smiled, and said, "Weird I get the pity kindness again, but I'm happy for it, actually."

"It wasn't pity. I would do anything to make your dreams possible now, and if you can make my dreams possible I would like that as well.

We help each other out, because we're friends, and that's what friends do." I said, "So what about Dragon Guy? You think he's gonna win the popular vote?"

Malena said, "I believe with all my heart he will. He is very charismatic, a true gentleman, with a wild side that you can't say no to. He will be a great ruler. It's a shame he paid so heartily, even though I would've liked to have given him a discount, or even just free love, but I think it will help him in the long run knowing that love is not free. There is always a price, our souls, bodies, and very heart. Everything is on the line, in love, and we trade it to receive it again."

49

Anke said, when the others came to meet Malena and I, "We saw Tas sneaking around outside the hostel. I could tell that she had a gun underneath her coat... She always does that, that one thing, when she is in 'work mode...'"

I said, "Yeah, Luke gets that thing, that one thing, that facial expression, when he draws me. He looks so serious! I mean, he's seeing women naked, for Christ's sake! He should be happy."

Anke said, "Tas looked like a whole different person. Like a killer, in actuality. I think we should leave for a while... I really don't want to fight the Madame as weak as we all are, and I don't want to fight Tas."

Francesca held Malena's hand, and said, "...You really look nice, Malena."

Malena smiled, and Francesca squeezed her hand before letting go.

I looked at Malena, and said, "...Let's job dodge a little bit longer. How about we go camping now. Sound good, everyone?"

They all agreed, and we got the hospital, after a bit of paperwork and a lot of convincing from Francesca, since Francesca knew the most how to work systems of any kind, to let Malena go with us on a camping trip. It was healthiest for her, anyway, continuing her life and not being trapped in a hospital til the end of her days.

We took Malena's car, and bought tents, blankets, a little gas stove, and food to add to our supplies, then ditched Holland down the road to Germany, to go camping where Malena wanted, the Black Forest of Germany.

Luke took Malena out of the car, and set her down in a wheelchair in our camping site. Malena stroked his arms gently, and said to him, "You have such strength."

Luke gently said, "I used to be a wild man, working out whenever I could. I took athletic sports, fighting sports, in my younger days. I walked for miles and miles, also running down the road. I'm not as strong as I was then… but the lingering strength serves me well."

Malena said, "I am very happy for you. I cannot accumulate strength, besides very, very gradually. My legs do not work, my arms are weak. Even the internals can be damaged if I am jostled forcefully. Thank you for being so gentle with your strength."

Luke wheeled Malena to the fire pit, and made a fire for her, starting a fire with his lighter, as we set up the tents.

We all just drank and laughed, especially Malena, and I could hear other people in the campsites having fun as well. I looked at the next campsite over, and saw a Japanese woman and a short man hugging, and then the short man went to the tent. The albino woman with her talked for a bit, and eventually the albino went to the tent as well.

I decided to offer this woman a beer, this Japanese stranger, and went over to her fire.

"Hi. I noticed you guys are having fun! Want a beer? You can join us if you like. My name's Jane." I said, shaking her hand.

The woman looked surprised, and said, "Nevaeh. I can see that you're an American like me! Cool. Yeah, I'll come over for a bit. Thanks for the beer, dude."

Luke, Anke, Malena, Francesca, and I all laughed with Nevaeh. She was quite a charming individual! Luke and her talked about writing, as

Nevaeh was once a journalist and now working on her first book. Anke and Nevaeh were so snarky to each other, in a silly way, and Francesca asked Nevaeh, "So you lost your job, too?"

Nevaeh said, "Well, it sort of lost me. It just wasn't what I wanted to do anymore, and I am actually much happier writing for myself, than stupid pieces in the paper."

Francecsa said, "You inspire me. I think… you all inspire me. I would like to draw by the fire, and later, I will work on a romantic comedy of my own. Something to make me feel happy."

Francesca drew by the fireside to herself, and Nevaeh asked Malena, "So what's your story? You've been awfully quiet."

Malena said, "…I have? I don't know. I just did not want to intrude on everyone's conversation."

"Kinda weird. You're like the elephant in the room. You don't see much cripples going camping. I like that, and it's pretty neat that you're doing things people wouldn't expect." Nevaeh said.

Malena blushed, and said, "I am happy to meet travelers like you. It's something that really made me feel good, in my old job."

"You were what, a secretary?" Nevaeh asked.

"I was a prostitute." Malena said.

Nevaeh opened her eyes wide, and said, "…Is… Is that safe, for you? In America… it's not a good thing to be a prostitute. I don't know about these legal Euro prostitutes, but…"

Malena smiled, and said, "I used to look differently, back then."

Nevaeh said, "…Ah. I'm sure you can find a better job, too."

Malena said, "I don't really care about my work, anymore… I just want to find love, finally. One day, I hope."

Nevaeh sighed, and said, "Yeah, I get that. I lost so many loves… Now I'm bumming with my friends, a real lovey dovey couple, just to pass the time. Men are idiots, and I suggest just finding a good friend first, and then the love will follow."

Malena said, "A good friend? But I thought of all of them as my friend, in some degree."

Nevaeh said, "Well, it's like this, at least in the story I've been writing. We lust after people who may not be perfect for us, but instead the main character's *true* love is once her enemy. Love blossoms, stuff happens… but she loses that love again. Instead of wallowing in grief for her love's death, however, she meets good friends who just show love in themselves, even without sex. It's the friends who are our real loves, and not what we do in the bed."

Malena said, "I like that. I am very tired, so could you take me to my sleeping bag, Luke? I want to tell you all that I love you, very much."

Luke smiled, picked her up, and brought her to her sleeping bag in the tent, letting her sleep the night.

We drank and joked for a bit more, all of us besides Malena, and then went to bed as the fire was dwindling to nothing, Francesca now writing story ideas down on paper, next to a picture of someone she could love.

50

We took Malena back to the hospital, so that they could eventually have her be independent enough to live comfortably. Malena thanked us, and said, "Confront your fears. Show the Madame that we can love whoever we want, and that she cannot make us do anything awful. You are not evil, Mary, you are a saint, Anke, you have all the power you ever needed already, Francesca, and Luke… take care of your muses."

We each hugged her goodbye, and she waved a hand weakly, gently, at us as we left the room. We didn't really want to leave, as the doctors and nurses came out, but we allowed them to both get to work, Malena and the hospital, and would visit her again soon.

Francesca said, as we passed down the halls of the hospital, "I'd take her back home with me, back to Britain, if she wanted. I could care for her, love her as she likes, and do all that… but it feels like she wouldn't accept my care, if she can figure out a way to care for herself independently. She's strong."

Anke said, "So… lose your virginity, and then you fall in love? It's a good thing your first time was with Malena… because that is always a stupid choice, and I'm sure Malena can let you down easily."

Francesca blushed, and said, "Well, I'm not gay or anything, and she was a man when we did it, but I don't know… I feel like I owe her, or something. She was just so… so nice."

Anke said, "That's why you don't sample your own goods, Francesca, you'll get hooked. Oh well. None of us are going to be working prostitution, hopefully ever again in my opinion, so I guess you'll have to go to the competition."

Francesca said, "I honestly would, but I... am absolutely broke. *Everything* I accumulated under the Madame is now the Madame's. I even checked out my bank account, and it was completely empty, as it was under the Madame as well... I'm glad that I can mooch off you guys, just for a bit."

Anke said, "Don't worry about it... I think we can let you mooch for a good while, and we can vanish into the folds of the world together, for a while, as soon as I take what's mine back from the Madame as well... Tas."

Francesca said, "I'm glad you two... care for each other, so well these days. You always did flirt, jokingly because you were both 'women,' so I'm glad you don't need to make jokes anymore."

Anke sighed, and said, "I just hope she's not going to kill us all if the Madame says so. I know you all think Tas is a kind, nice, loving person, but... she was a mercenary, a soldier, and I don't know if you've ever seen war movies... but soldiers don't play the good guys in real life. If you wanted to get an accurate description of who Tas really is when she works, look at both sides of the war in those movies, lump them together, add a hint of street smarts, and you've got Tas."

Luke said, "Maybe really she's just like those old war comedy TV shows? Hitting each other on the head gently and making jokes?"

Anke said, "Sorry, Luke. I know you've got a thing for her... but she's killed a lot of people who have messed with our businesses, and I don't know how many as she was growing up. One time I was beaten as I was in a job, this was when I was new and still getting the hang of my powers, and after the Madame gave the order, the guy lost his hands, and penis for insurance. No one knows about the brutality of our work, but just because it is legal, doesn't mean it can also not be criminal.

"Of course, we're always the good guys, we play that part. We're the poor prostitute just trying to have a go at life again, and revenge is looked at as acceptable if you hurt one of us. Really, when laying with a prostitute, you are risking your life as well as your cash, because there's always the pimp in the next room... waiting to hear me scream.

"I was merchandise, a cash cow, property. I accepted this illusion, even though I knew I was a human being with the same freedom as any other.

"The Madame was our pimp, our Madame, our boss. Doesn't matter if she's female, magical, really old, or whatever. She was just a pimp, and Tas is her thug."

Luke said, "...So how come you two care for each other so much?"

Anke said, "Because I am a human being, and Tas is one too. Just because we aren't the best humans doesn't mean we're not still human. She cares, she doesn't want to take a life, and that's why she's good at it. If she was a sadist she wouldn't be efficient. I love her as a human being, and I know she loves me too."

We had no weapons. Would any weapon do us any good? We got before the house, and I knocked on the door.

Tas answered, with a stony look in her eyes. She said, "Please come in, we are under renovations right now, as some of our staff are missing... but you lot know that well, don't you."

Anke went first, to hug Tas, but Tas stepped back and opened the door wider. Anke put down her arms, and we walked inside the house.

We then noticed the pistol in Tas's hand.

She was holding it comfortably, gently, and almost... like one of our talismans. A completely mundane talisman, with completely mundane power.

A very deadly looking gun.

51

We got to the Madame's office, Tas at our back with the pistol at her side, ready to use it if necessary, and we saw a very pretty young girl walk out of the Madame's office, smiling in glee and holding a fantastic looking ebony wand.

My heart fell to my stomach, and I told her, "Please. Leave this place, now."

She looked at me quizzically, and said, "Why? I have so much power! I can feel this place crackle with dreams and strength! I can't wait to start working!"

I said, "Please, tell me your name. I'm Mary Jane."

She looked at me even more confused, and said, "It's… It's… hmm… I guess it's a secret! I'm going to pick a new work name, see ya!" and she walked off down the halls, humming a happy tune.

Tas said, "That's your replacement, Abbot. She's completely brand new, saving herself just to get that extra losing her virginity cash. She can clean up after herself well, too, and we're thinking we never even needed a maid."

Anke said, "You know the whole losing your virginity lay is a scam we do!! And it's Anke!"

Tas said, "Well, it'll come out a lot more convincing when it's actually real, and not an illusion. You can call yourself whoever you like, Abbot, but I just like calling you Abbot. Please, Luke... The Madame wants to discuss the interview artistry of yours."

Luke looked pale, and was about to enter the room, but I quickly held hands with Luke, and stared Tas hard in the eyes in fury. Tas just waved a hand for me to go in as well.

We sat in the chairs in front of the Madame's desk.

I saw her for what she was, when I looked into her eyes.

The tentacles... the teeth...

But I wasn't scared of her as much as I was before.

Oh, who am I kidding, I was terrified, but I still stared at her hard back in the eyes.

The Madame smiled, and said to Luke, "I'd like to buy your work, now. This grand playbook of us, this beautiful craftsmanship of words and art. I would like to offer you a fortune in wealth, with your name on the cover, displaying our lovely, attractive house.

"But I've noticed something in your work. You don't ever mention the name of the house."

Luke smiled nervously, and said, "W-Well, I really think the people behind the house are the true heroes, and not the house itself."

The Madame said, "Well... If you just put in our name, sign this contract, then we can go into business together for real. You never have to be a struggling, independent artist again, and you can have the house and all your friends at your side, instead."

I said, "Do not tempt him, *Magdalene.* You sound like my father."

Mary Magdalene looked at me, grimaced, and said, "I do? Oh, I'm sorry... I guess I can take after him sometimes, with him haunting my footsteps as well as yours. The Devil was always amongst us, Mary Jane, ready to destroy us at any time. You are simply proof of that."

"No matter your seduction, threats, or intimidation, we will not bow down to *you.*" I said.

"This is the contract, Luke, I hope you read it well, and find the terms satisfactory." the Madame said, and gave Luke a piece of paper.

Luke skimmed through it, gulped, and put the paper back down.

He said, "I think I'd have to hire an agent... probably a lawyer too, just to have this looked at... Mary Jane? Care to be my agent? What do you think of this deal?"

He handed the paper to me, and I burned it to nothing in my hand.

The Madame sighed, and said, "I suppose you will always be independent... painfully alone. Very. Well. Keep the name of the house out of your work, then, or there will be legal scandals, coming straight for you."

Luke sighed.

I said, "And I suppose, you yourself lost your name as well, Magdalene, because you could not come to terms with an artist. Your house's name will only go down in whispered rumors, and never be uttered aloud."

Magdalene said, "I suppose. I can always start another, in a few centuries, that will be remembered much better. I do not hold any of you to your past responsibilities, and allow you to walk away freely... Allow me to continue my work, dears. There are so many more people to *enslave.*"

We went pale, and walked out of the room.

Tas said to us in the hall, "I told you I'm not the good guy. We break our binds, to put on other ones. We were always slaves, servants of someone, even almighty God. It is much nicer when we choose the bindings."

I asked Tas, "Why?! What binding does she have on you??"

Tas said, "Freedom, for me, and others. We have freedom and power here, love and acceptance, cash whenever we need it. This is the life, Mary Jane, and I never want to go back to my old one, afraid, confused, starving, poor... and alone."

Anke said, "We're going to talk, Tas."

At the bar, our last drinks here, Anke was breaking up with Tas. Anke said, "This is not a threat, or a negotiation, or some tactic. I'm breaking up with you, Tas."

Tas said, "...But, please, can't we still see each other, even because of my work? You all don't have to continue at it, and can do whatever you like! I love you, Abbot."

Anke said, "My name is Anke Abbot, and I dreamed of making you Tas Abbot as well. I love you... but our time is done."

Tas said, "...What if I quit? Give up working with the Madame?"

Anke said, "That's your choice, Tas. It won't have any bearing on our relationship."

Tas said, "...And this isn't some sort of trick, or illusion, or some gimmick?"

Anke sighed, and said, "The whole thing was an illusion, and I fooled myself with it. Do you want to know why illusions still leave remnants behind? It's because the people who see them believe they are real. You will leave a very big hole in my heart, but I can let it heal."

Tas put her hands to her face, took them away, and said, "I want to believe it is an illusion, though."

Anke held Tas's hand and said, "You always did want to be a soldier, Tas. You were only ever one for me. You are not a soldier to the Madame, you are a hook up artist, a bouncer, a bodyguard, a drug dealer, and a thug. That is the truth."

Tas went pale.

Anke continued, "I will never love you again, as long as you are in love with this illusion. I will always be your friend, and we will remain so for the rest of our days. But I think we should... just be friends."

You could see the heartbreak from across the room, from where Francesca, Luke and I were seated, the heartbreak from both parties.

Tas got up, looked like she wanted to stay, and then left the bar.

Anke burst out crying, and we came up to her to comfort her.

We heard the gunshot from outside, Anke looked up from crying, and screamed.

52

They were rushing Tas to the hospital, after she tried to take her own life.

She tried to shoot herself in the heart, and it looked like she hit it, but I believe missed.

They were still operating on her, and we stayed with Malena as Anke shook.

We were all worried, scared, because they told us the truth that Tas doesn't have much of a chance to live.

I sighed, and said I'll go as quickly as I could to talk to someone who could help.

I opened the window in Malena's room, burst out my wings, and flew to the house.

I landed before the Madame, who was just sitting outside and enjoying the stars.

She said to me, "Every one of those beautiful sparkles fills me with dread… because I know I'm going to have to look at them for the rest of my life, even as the world collapses, there will still be stars."

"Please help us cure Tas. They say she won't last." I said.

"You want me to steal someone's death? You could bring her to life again, you know." Magdalene said.

"I know that will be a mistake. I know you can make things rectifiable, rectifiable enough." I said, standing before her.

"I've learned as a prostitute, in my past, that you do not give away the experience of life for free. I learned as a Madame that this experience can be traded, for far greater power. I will accept your deal, Mary Jane, if you will accept mine. You will destroy magic, and with it the world." Magdalene said.

"But that will just kill Tas again!! Destroying the world will kill everyone!!" I said.

"It is your choice. Which is more favorable? One life for a bit longer, or the rest? A life you love, care for, and is a friend? Would you trade the world for this life?" Magdalene said.

"...Yes. I will do as you ask. Now fix Tas." I said.

Magdalene opened her eyes wide, and said, "She is now better, as the doctor has just figured out how to save her life, in a spectacular, once in a lifetime manner. She will go down as a hero in her profession, live a long, successful life in medicine, and Tas will live again."

"...How do I know you even did anything??" I asked.

"You have faith, like you should've for Tas." Magdalene said.

I slumped my shoulders, and said, "I accept this faith. What is it you want me to do?"

"Bring the rats from the gutters, bring the dead to life, have the horse*women* of the apocalypse at your side, and bring an end.

"This is the end of my story, and I will watch the next one in glee. I abandon this paltry ruse, this whorehouse without a name, and look forth to what will await.

"If you ever need me again... I advise you to pray, instead of call on powers inconceivable.

"Good luck, Mary Jane. I'll see you in the next story." Mary Magdalene said, and walked down the road, away from the house.

I looked at the house, and it was always abandoned, no one there, not even the chef, besides one pretty woman with an ebony wand losing her virginity to a rather ugly tourist.

53

Over the next few weeks, Anke, Francesca, Malena, Luke and I visited with Tas. Tas could barely hold consciousness, and had a wonked out expression from all the pain medicine.

Two others joined us as well, who decided to visit the Madame and thank her for all her care, but when they looked for the Madame, she had disappeared.

Diane said to us, "It is very strange, like no one can even remember her, and she never existed. I believe we have been blessed with a very unique experience."

John said, "Fuckin milf is probably the holiest cunt alive, her and that... what's it... the doc who sewed me together. I hated that evil hand sewing me up at the start... but... now I am so happy." and held hands with Diane.

I looked at Diamond's steel scalpel in my hand. It continued to whisper, telling me the horrors it had done. It sounded like every other voice I heard.

For now, it told me of Tas's pain, as Diamond cut off her penis. Of course when it happened Tas was numb, completely, albeit cruelly conscious, but still... the losing of that genitalia, being in the middle with nothing for a little bit, was terrifying for her.

Tas mumbled, "Whaaaa? Am I here... or there?? I saaaawww... so mannnny lighttts... I feel sooo happppyyyy..."

Anke said, "Do you feel like playing cards, Tas?"

Tas said, "Oooohhhh... Yes. Let's play fish."

Anke said, "Go Fish it is, Tas." and sighed, shuffling a deck.

Francesca said to me, "...So what the Madame said, who says she's Mary Magdalene... is that we're *all* harbingers of the apocalypse??"

"I guess." I said, "Although I think everyone can be a harbinger if they want to. I wouldn't worry about it... I have no intention of-"

Tas said, "Goooo fisssshhhh..." and flat lined.

The doctors immediately came in again and worked on her, as Anke sat in the corner and we left. The cards had fallen to the floor.

Anke had been crying relentlessly, and she cried again as Tas reclaimed consciousness.

Anke said to us, "Please allow me and Tas to get some rest. I will speak to you all later, but I am so worried right now."

I hugged her goodbye, and we went to Francesca's pad, once Luke's studio. Luke decided he'd like to go home after all this, with me, and I agreed. Malena was allowed to come with us back to the pad.

Francesca said, "Well. I guess I've gotta sell this place. It was nice... but I can't really afford it, and having that little bit of cash will make it easier to navigate life again."

Luke said, "I'm surprised you even allowed me to stay, even though you had ulterior motives for letting me do so. I suppose you at least have a little something to your name."

Francesca laughed half heartedly, and said, "I'm moving back in with my parents... I'm going to have a go at what I want to do in life, rather than what will make me money. It will be worth it, I think."

Malena said, "I will be going too, Francesca."

Francesca did a double take at Malena, and said, "Really?? You make me so happy, Malena." and Francesca hugged the crippled woman in a wheelchair, and Malena gently hugged her back.

Diane and John were sitting silently, holding hands, but Diane said, "I have no home, not even with the Madame now. I would like to travel some more, with my immense savings, but I hope to check in on all of you at some point in your and my life."

I asked Diane, "So really the Madame had no hold on you? Can you remember your name, use magic?"

Diane said, "I never had a name. I was always a slave. The Madame did not take from me, she gave. Magic will give as it takes, and I have power that I never could... Plants are agreeable, in most every scenario, and my power stems from life and not objects. I could seek the Madame out... but it is our arrangement, to not go poking into each other's heads when we do not need to.

"You believe she tricked you all, stole something from you, but perhaps she gave it back to you, when you tried to lose it.

"Anke had no love, not even a family name. But she found so much more in Tas, and found her family with her father and us. She only needed to accept that, like her name, and she has all she ever wanted.

"You, Francesca, have so much power... Intellect up the wazoo, and beauty besides. You used this for endless gain, remarkably so... but in the end it all meant nothing, and your drive was misplaced. Now you are working for what you love, and not what you desire.

"Mary, you came here for one purpose, to learn of power and magic, the supernatural and your roots. You have found that it really is a pointless fascination, and real magic can be found just as much in the mundane, like with your artist.

"And Malena... I know it is difficult reclaiming your body, but there are advancements in medicine every day, and maybe you will even walk again. Your heart wasn't only physically in your body, your heart was always with us, with the love you dole out relentlessly.

"And Tas has her life again, as *she* desires, maybe a true life even after all of this.

"Of course, I am being optimistic, and trying to find lesson in hardship, but that is the way of life… It's one, giant, messed up lesson without an end.

"I hope you have all learned something, at the Madame's school, as I have."

54

Luke and I talked on the airplane back home, making jokes and digesting this entire journey.

"So which one of you is the first, Conquest, then?" Luke said.

"Hmm... Gotta say Anke Abbot. Sometimes that one is the antichrist, and no one so profane and holy than Anke." I said.

"I thought that would be you, cuz, you know. Devil's Daughter." Luke said.

"Nahh... I'm too blunt to pose as Christ. That was the Madame's one flaw in her plan, trying to turn me into someone I'm not." I said.

"So, now War." Luke said.

"Hmm... Malena. She wielded a physical knife as her talisman. She is at war with the world, with her body, although her true power is love." I said.

Luke smiled, and said, "Famine?"

"Francesca. She gave all those people pork rinds! And she can take them as well. That one's got something to do with paying for something, right?" I said.

"That one holds scales, taking all instead. I can see that being Francesca and her businesses." Luke said.

"I gotta say Death is Tas... She is the most dangerous, dealing and then almost receiving death. And she's got Hell following behind her, watching her back... All of us." I said.

"So which character do you represent?" Luke asked.

"Duh! The Devil's Daughter! I represent myself, and if an apocalypse happens, I sure as heck am not following some silly old Bible. I'm gonna put my own twist on the whole thing. Diane can be our morale booster, as we destroy the Earth. She's so good at that, for some reason." I said.

Luke sighed, and said, "It's going to be so nice being back home."

"I know, Luke. I love you, and our home." I said.

"I love you too, Mary Jane." Luke said, and we kissed in our seats.

The End

See you
Soon!

www.ingramcontent.com/pod-product-compliance
Lightning Source LLC
Chambersburg PA
CBHW070338200726
48294CB00003B/707